Tears misted her eyes. Elena had never believed she could love someone so much it hurt.

"Something's wrong," Jed said gently, a slight frown pulling dark brows together now. "Tell me, my darling."

She couldn't! Not yet, not until she could get her own head around it. And even then it would be almost impossible.

"Not really—it's just that what we have frightens me, Jed." And that, at least, was the truth.

She had joyfully accepted the gift of their love for each other with both eager hands. But it frightened her now because she was afraid they were going to lose it, that his love for her wouldn't be strong enough to cope with what she was going to have to tell him....

DIANA HAMILTON

The Unexpected Baby

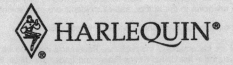

TORONTO • NEW YORK • LONDON
AMSTERDAM • PARIS • SYDNEY • HAMBURG
STOCKHOLM • ATHENS • TOKYO • MILAN • MADRID
PRAGUE • WARSAW • BUDAPEST • AUCKLAND

ISBN 0-373-12041-9

THE UNEXPECTED BABY

First North American Publication 1999.

Copyright © 1999 by Diana Hamilton.

CHAPTER ONE

'WHAT took you so long?' Jed's eyes gleamed with sultry promise beneath heavy half-closed lids, his gorgeous mouth curving sensually as he invited, 'Come back to bed, Mrs Nolan. And take that thing off. Pretty it may be, but your body's a darn sight prettier.'

Elena couldn't meet his eye. She felt sick. She told herself it was shock, or auto-suggestion. She stuffed her hands in the side pockets of the silk wrap she'd dragged on before leaving the bathroom so he wouldn't see how much they were trembling.

Her mouth went dry just looking at him. He was her love, her life, everything. He made her feel special, secure, treasured.

The sheet tangled around his lean hips was the only thing between him and total nakedness. Six foot three of superbly honed masculinity, with a sizzling, white-hot sexual magnetism that jumped out and hit her. For a thirty-six-year-old business man—a shopkeeper, Sam had once half mockingly described him—he had the body of an athlete and a face that only just missed classical perfection, courtesy of a slight bump at the bridge of his nose—broken on the rugby field—and a tough, pugnacious jaw.

Sam's name in her mind made her want to scream. How could she have been so reckless? She had thought she'd known what she was doing, when in reality she'd known nothing at all, just gone ahead in her usual pig-headed fashion, wanting it all. Everything.

And how could she bring herself to break the news to Jed? Put something like that into the pure beauty of their marriage? The short answer was she couldn't. Not yet, anyway. Not while the irrefutable evidence was a scant ten minutes old, burning holes in her brain.

Her heart punched savagely at her breastbone as with a whimper of distress she discarded her wrap, flew impulsively to the bed and flung herself down beside him. Wrapping her body around him, she whispered with soft ferocity, 'I love you... I love you...'

'Still? After a whole week of marriage?'

Teasing silver lights danced deep in his lazily hooded eyes as he smoothed the long golden silk of her hair away from her face, and Elena said, her voice tight with anguish, 'Don't mock me, Jed. Don't!'

'As if!' His smile was soft, melting her, as he eased her onto her back, propping himself up on one elbow, his beautifully proportioned body half covering hers. Thick dark hair tumbled over his forehead, the curve of his mouth a sinful seduction as he gently rubbed his thumb over her full lips.

Tears misted her eyes. She had never believed she could love someone so much it hurt. Or that she could ever be this afraid. For ten years she had been afraid of no one, and nothing. She'd known what she wanted and sweated blood to get it. And now, because of a moment of reckless, arrogant folly, she had turned herself into a frightened wreck, full of dread.

'Something's wrong,' he said gently, a slight frown

pulling dark brows together now. 'Tell me, my darling.'

She couldn't! Not yet, not until she could get her own head around it. And even then it would be almost impossible. Hating having to lie to him, even by omission, despising the way her voice shook, she muttered, 'Not really—its just that what we have frightens me, Jed.' And that, at least, was the truth.

It hadn't frightened her before; she had joyfully accepted the gift of their love for each other with both eager hands. But it frightened her now because she was afraid they were going to lose it, that his love for her wouldn't be strong enough to cope with what she was going to have to tell him.

The unbelievably precious gift of their love had come so quickly, so easily. She'd been too deliriously happy to imagine that it could be taken from her just as suddenly.

She swallowed the knot of aching tears in her throat and said thickly, trying to lighten the sombre darkness she could see in his eyes, 'You see, I still can't believe you could have fallen in love with a thirty-year-old divorcee when you could have had just about anyone!' She tried to smile, and failed, and closed her eyes instead. Her heart threatened to burst as she felt his lips kiss the tears away from her spangled lashes.

'I didn't want just anyone,' he assured her, his voice huskily tender. 'But I wanted you from the first moment I saw you. The circumstances couldn't have been more dire, but I already felt I knew you from what Sam had told me, and I took one look at you and knew I wanted to be with you for the rest of my life.'

That had been six short weeks ago, when she'd travelled from her home here in Spain to England for Sam's funeral. And despite the terrible, numbing sadness of the occasion, with the raw early-April wind that had scoured the small Hertfordshire graveyard adding to the misery, she had taken one look at Sam's elder brother and known she had found the only man who could make her break her vow never to become emotionally dependent on any man ever again.

Just one look and her life had changed; she had changed.

Jed eased himself down beside her and drew her bright head into the angle of his shoulder, holding her as if she were the most precious thing in the world. 'I didn't want one of the glossy harpies that crowd the social scene with monotonous regularity—shallow and superficial, the sort of woman whose main interest in a man is the size of his bank balance. I wanted *you*. Talented, successful, a self-made woman—heart-wrenchingly beautiful. And scorchingly sexy is the icing on the cake, the ribbon on the package! And from what you've told me, you're well rid of the man you married when you were little more than a child. What was it? Barely nineteen years of age? Sweetheart, everyone's allowed to make one mistake, and he was yours!'

One mistake? What about this latest one? Would he dismiss it with such compassionate understanding?

If only they hadn't rushed into marriage; if only she hadn't believed there would be no consequences after what she and Sam had done—hadn't believed she was right in dismissing the possible repercussions of that one last night, when wine, the heady promise of the beginning of the early Spanish spring, the feeling that something was missing in her successful life and an overdose of sentimentality had led to something that could poison her whole relationship with the man who had taught her to recognise the depths and strengths of a love she had never before even guessed she was capable of.

She turned her head and feverishly kissed his warm, hair-roughened skin, searching for the flat male nipples, the palms of her hands splayed against the heat of his skin, her fingers digging into the suddenly taut muscles of his stomach. She heard the passionate inhalation of his breath, felt the responsive surge of his body and swallowed hot, salt tears. She would not cry. She would not!

There could be few such precious moments left to them.

When his mouth took hers it was a statement of passionate possession, and she answered it with the fire of her need, her adoration, curling her legs around him, opening for him, accepting him eagerly, answering the fevered stroke of his hands as they caressed her body with a feverish exploration of her own.

She felt the intensity of his rapture as he possessed her, and she lost herself in their loving, fear forgotten, just for now, just for the slow, exquisitely languorous time of his loving, just while they drove each other to the outer limits of ecstasy. She rained wild kisses on the hot skin of his throat, felt the wild beat of his heart and clung to this, this perfection, because maybe it would be the very last time for them.

*   *   *

'I could get used to this!'

Despite her bare feet, Jed must have heard her walk out of the whitewashed stone house onto the patio. Or felt her presence, she decided with a shiver of recognition, just as she always sensed his nearness before she actually saw him.

The black T-shirt he was wearing was tucked into the pleated waistband of a pair of stone-grey tough cotton trousers. The way he looked—lithe, lean and dangerously male—rocked her senses as he turned from the low wall that divided the patio from the sun-drenched, steeply sloping gardens below. 'And just in case you think I'm a cheapskate, saving on honeymoon expenses by using my bride's home as a hotel, I've made breakfast.'

Coffee, a bowl of fresh fruit, crispy rolls and a dish of olives. Half her brain approved his efforts while the other half gloried in the warmth of his smile, in the unashamed, naked hunger in his eyes. 'Though I might do without,' he added. 'Food, that is. You look good enough to eat. You satisfy each and every one of what I've discovered to be amazingly huge appetites!'

Did she? Elena's aquamarine eyes locked onto his, warm colour flaring briefly over her high cheekbones. Every moment was doubly precious now, every word spoken with love to be treasured, because very soon now it would end.

After her shower she'd pulled on a pair of frayed-edged denim shorts and an old white T-shirt, not taking any trouble because half an hour ago, when he'd slid out of bed, she'd feigned sleep, needing just a little time on her own to decide what to do. And she'd faced the awful knowledge that it was no use waiting until the time was right before she introduced the serpent into their corner of paradise.

The time would never be right for what she had to tell him, and keeping the truth from him would only make him think more badly of her.

But the way he was looking at her, the way his eyes slid over every last one of her five-foot-six slender inches and endless, elegant, lightly tanned legs, paralysed her with physical awareness. So, despising her weakness but unable to do anything about it, she took his former remark and clung to it as to a reprieve. Just a few more hours. Surely she could give herself that?

Striving for lightness as she poured coffee for them both, she told him, 'Stop fishing for compliments— there's nothing cheapskate about you! I practically forced you to agree to spend our honeymoon here.'

She was justifiably proud of her home. She'd bought the former Andalucian farmhouse with part of the proceeds from the sale of the film rights of her first runaway bestseller. And she and Jed had already decided to keep it as a holiday home, to come here as often as they could—a welcome respite from the pressure of his position at the head of the family-owned business. Based in London, Amsterdam, New York and Rome, it had a two-hundred-year-old tradition of supplying sumptuous gems and exquisitely wrought precious metals to the seriously wealthy.

Sam had considered the business arcane, refused to have anything to do with it, making his mark in the highly competitive world of photo-journalism.

She pushed his name roughly out of her head, but,

almost as if he'd known what she'd done, Jed pushed
it straight back in again. 'I can understand why Sam
came here so often between assignments. Life travels
at a different pace, the views are endless and the sun
is generous. He told me once that it was the only place
he could find peace.'

He refilled his coffee cup and tipped the pot towards
her, one dark brow lifting. Elena shook her head. She
had barely taken a sip. Listening to him talking of his
brother was screwing up her nerves and shredding
them. Why should he decide to talk about him now?
She couldn't meet his eyes.

Jed replaced the pot, selected an orange from the
blue earthenware bowl and began to strip away the
peel, his voice strangely clipped as he remarked, 'Over
the last couple of years, particularly, he was always
getting sent to the world's worst trouble spots. Though
I think he thrived on the edge of danger, he must have
been grateful for the relaxation he knew he could find
here. With you. He seemed to know so much about
you; you must have been extremely close.'

Elena's throat closed up. He had rarely mentioned
Sam's name since the day of his funeral, but now the
very real grief showed through. The brothers had had
very little in common but they had loved each other.
And now she could detect something else. Something
wildly out of character. A skein of jealousy, envy,
even?

'He was a good friend,' she responded, hating the
breathless catch in her voice. She watched the long,
hard fingers strip the peel from the fruit. Suddenly
there seemed something ruthless about the move-

ments. She wondered if she knew him as thoroughly as she'd thought she did.

She shivered, and heard him say, 'In a way, I think he deplored the fact that I did my duty, as he called it—knuckled down and joined the family business and took the responsibility of heading it after Father died—despised me a little, even.'

'No!' She couldn't let him think that. 'He admired you, and respected you—maybe grudgingly—for doing your duty, and doing it so well. He once told me that your business brain scared the you-know-what out of him, and that he preferred to go off and do his own thing rather than live in your shadow, a pale second-best.'

Jed gave her a long, searching look, as if he was turning her words over in his mind, weighing the truth of them, before at last admitting, 'I didn't know that. Maybe I wouldn't have envied him his freedom to do as he pleased and to hell with everyone else if I had.' Regret tightened his mouth. 'I guess there's a whole raft of things I didn't know about my kid brother. Except, of course, how fond he was of you. When he came home on those flying visits of his the conversation always came round to you. He gave me one of your books and told me to be impressed. I was; I didn't need telling,' he complimented coolly. 'You handle horror with a sophistication, intelligence and subtlety that makes a refreshing change from the usual crude blood and gore of the genre.'

'Thank you.' I think, she added to herself. There was something in his voice she had never heard before. Something dark and condemning. She left her seat swiftly and went to lean against the wall, looking at the endless view which always soothed her spirits but signally failed to do anything of the sort this morning.

Perched on a limestone ridge, high above a tiny white-walled village, her home benefited from the pine-scented salt breezes crossing western Andalucia from the Atlantic, moderating the heat of the burning May sun.

Elena closed her eyes and tried to close her mind to everything but the cooling sensation of the light wind on her face. Just a few moments of respite before she had to face the truth, brace herself to break the news to Jed before the day ended. Could she use her gift for words to make him understand just why she had acted as she had? It didn't seem possible, she thought defeatedly.

Since the ending of her first disastrous marriage, she had refused to let anything defeat her, get in the way of her fight for successful independence. But this— this was something else...

'You haven't eaten a thing.' He'd come to stand behind her, not touching but very close. The heat of his body scorched her, yet she shivered. 'Not hungry? Suddenly lost your appetite?'

His cool tones terrified her. He hadn't already guessed, had he? No, of course he hadn't. How could he? Despising herself for the way she seemed to be heading—spoiling the morning and the few hours' respite she'd promised herself—she turned and forced a smile to the mouth she had always considered far too wide.

'No, just lazy, I guess.' She walked back to the table. She would have to force something into a stomach that felt as if it would reject anything she tried to feed it. 'I thought we might go down to the coast today.' She plucked a few grapes from the dewy bunch nestling in the fruit bowl. 'Cadiz, perhaps, or Vejer de la Frontera if you fancy somewhere quieter. We haven't set foot outside the property all week.'

Edgy, acutely aware of the way he was watching her, she popped a grape into her mouth and felt her throat close up as he answered, 'So far, we haven't felt the need to, remember?'

She bit on the grape and forced it down, because she could hardly spit the wretched thing out. His words had been idly spoken, yet the underlining accusation came through loud and clear. They hadn't needed to leave the property; they'd had all they needed in each other. Simple expeditions through the gardens and into the pine woods, eating on the patio or in the rose-covered arbour, their lives attuned to the wonderful solitude, the rhythm of their lovemaking, the deep rapture of simply being. Together.

'Of course I do.' Her voice was thick, everything inside her panicking. The incredible feeling of closeness, of being made for each other, was slipping away. She knew it would happen once she'd broken her news, but the frightening distance between them had no right to be happening now. It hadn't been there before he'd begun to talk of Sam. 'Pilar, who helps me around the house, was instructed to keep well clear after stocking the fridge on the morning we arrived.' She spoke as lightly as she could, desperate to recreate all that wonderful closeness for just a little longer. 'We're starting to run low on provisions, so I thought we could combine shopping with sightseeing, that's all.'

'Is it?' He prowled back to the chair opposite hers and sat, his hands clenched in the side pockets of his trousers. Steel-grey eyes searched her face. His voice was low, sombre, as he imparted, 'Sam and I had our differences, but he was my brother and I loved him. His death rocked me. Until coming here, to where he was happy, where he found peace and comfort, I haven't been able to open up about what I feel. Yet it seems to me that you don't want to talk about him. Get edgy when I mention his name. Why is that?' he wanted to know.

What to say? She couldn't deny it. She picked up her cup of now cold coffee and swallowed half of it down a throat that was aching with tension, and Jed asked tightly, 'Were you lovers? Is that the reason?'

Dread tore at her heart, knotted her stomach, perspiration dewing her forehead. For the first time since meeting him she deeply regretted his uncanny ability to see right into her soul. She twisted her hands in her lap and tried to smile.

'Why do you ask? Don't tell me you're trying to pick a fight!' Did her prevarication come out sounding as jokey as she'd intended? Or had she merely sounded as if she were being strangled?

'I ask because my talking about him appears to disturb you. It's something I never considered before, but from what I can gather Sam spent a fair amount of time here. He was a handsome son-of-a-gun. Add the spice of a dangerous occupation—no mere *shop-keeper*, our Sam—and an extremely beautiful woman with a talent he greatly admired, and what do you get?' He lifted one brow. 'I repeat the question.'

Elena felt everything inside her start to shake. Although Jed was doing his best to look relaxed and in control, his hands were still making fists in his side pockets, and that tough, shadowed jaw was tight. There was more to this than she could fully understand.

The fact that she'd been married before hadn't mattered to him. He hadn't wanted her to talk about it, had assimilated her, 'It was a dreadful mistake; he turned out to be completely rotten,' then refused to let her go on with the complete explanation she'd intended to make.

He'd dismissed her marriage to Liam Forrester as a total irrelevance, and had never once asked if there had been any other man in her life in the intervening years. He had acted as though their future was the only thing that was important to him.

Yet couple her name with Sam's and something suspiciously resembling jealousy and anger stared out of the eyes that had, thus far, only looked at her with love, warmth and hungry desire.

Because Sam had been his brother? Was there a twist of bitterness on that sensual mouth now? The sardonic stress he'd laid on the word 'shopkeeper' told her that Sam must have tossed that taunt at him at some time, told her that it still rankled.

And had Sam been handsome? Looking back, she supposed so. Not as tall as his brother, nothing like as powerfully built. Smooth, nut-brown hair and light blue eyes, with elegant features. He would have been a wow as an old-style matinée idol. Handsome he might have been, but he couldn't hold a candle to his older brother... Sam had had none of Jed's dangerous masculinity, none of that forbidding sexual excitement.

'Elena. I need to know.' There was a raw edge to his voice she had never heard before, and a few short hours ago she could have reassured him. But now, knowing what she knew, the task seemed impossible. Nevertheless, she had to try.

'I first met your brother at a party I threw to celebrate my second movie deal.' She concentrated on the facts because that was the only way she could handle this. 'I've made a lot of friends in this area—ex-pats as well as Spaniards. Sam came along with Cynthia and Ed Parry. He was staying with them for a few days—apparently he'd known Ed since university.'

She saw the way his brows pulled together, the way his mouth went tight, and knew he was turning over every word she said, impatient because she wasn't telling him what he wanted to know. But she had to do this her way, or not at all.

'That had to be about a couple of years ago,' she went on, needing him to see the whole thing from her perspective, needing to get it right. 'And, as you know, he often visited this corner of Spain when he needed to unwind. Usually he stayed with the Parrys—'

'But not always?'

'No,' she agreed, doing her best to stay calm, to ignore the churning, burning sensation in her tummy.

'We got to know each other well, enjoyed each other's company. He'd wander up here in the evenings and we'd talk, and sometimes, if it got very late, I'd offer him the use of one of the spare roms. You asked if we were lovers...' She lifted slender shoulders in a light shrug. 'He once admitted he had a low sex drive—something to do with using all his emotional and physical energy in his work. He knew the dangers of getting news out of the world's worst trouble spots. He talked a lot about you, your mother, your home. He was proud of his family. He told me he'd never marry, that such a commitment wouldn't be wise, or fair, because of the way he earned his living. But he said you would. Some woman to give you children because you wouldn't want the business to die out with you. Said that women flung themselves at you, couldn't keep away. But that you were picky. And discreet.'

Too late, she realised exactly what she was doing. And loathed herself for it. She had side-stepped his question and was trying to turn the situation round and become his accuser, letting the implication that he was a calculating user of women hang contentiously on the air between them, pushing them further apart.

And the bleak, most scornful look on his face told her he knew exactly what she was trying to do. And why.

Suddenly, the nausea that had been threatening all morning became an unwelcome, undeniable fact. She shot to her feet, one hand against her mouth, and lurched through the house to the bathroom.

Knowing he had followed her didn't help a scrap,

and when it was over she leant weakly against the tiled wall, the futile wish that she could turn the clock back three months uppermost in her mind.

'Sweetheart—come here.' He pulled her into his arms and she rested her throbbing head against the hard, soft-cotton-covered wall of his chest, wishing she could hold onto this moment for ever and knowing that she couldn't.

The look of compassion, of caring, on his face didn't help. It made things worse because she didn't deserve it. And when he said softly, 'What brought that on? Something you ate? I'll drive you to the nearest surgery if the sickness carries on,' she knew she had to tell him now.

Waking before him early this morning, she'd been rooting round at the back of the bathroom cabinet, looking for a fresh tube of toothpaste, when she'd found the pregnancy testing kit she'd bought.

Over the last few days she'd felt strangely nauseous on waking, had suffered one or two inexplicable dizzy spells. Common sense had told her that there were no repercussions from what she and Sam had done, but she'd run the test all the same, just to put her mind at rest.

And now she was going to have to face the consequences.

She pulled out of Jed's arms, her face white as she told him, 'I'm pregnant, Jed.'

Despite her ashen face, the dark torment in her eyes, he smiled at her, slowly shaking his head, one brow drifting up towards his hairline. He pulled her back against his body and enfolded her with loving arms.

The unresolved question of whether she and his brother had been more than good friends could wait.

'How can you possibly be sure of that, sweetheart? After only one week! It's a nice thought, but I'm afraid it's got to be something you ate!'

For a time she allowed herself the luxury of being held, waiting for her heartbeats to slow down to normal, for her aching head to stop whirling with stupid regrets. They'd discussed starting a family and decided there was no reason to wait. They both wanted children. Which was going to make what she had to tell him so much worse.

When she finally placed her hands against the powerful muscles of his chest and eased herself away from the haven of his embrace, she felt calm. Empty. She was about to tell him something he probably wouldn't want to live with, to kill his love, which was the most precious thing she had. She had to do it quickly and cleanly. The agony was too great to be prolonged.

'It's true, Jed. I did the test this morning.' She saw the look of disbelief on his face and knew he was about to tell her she'd got it wrong, misread the instructions. She forestalled him quickly, her voice thin because of the effort it took to control it. 'By my calculations, almost three months.'

And then she watched as his eyes froze over. 'Three months ago I hadn't met you, and the first time we had sex was on our wedding night,' he stated grimly, his lips thin and bloodless. 'So perhaps you'd like to tell me, my dear wife, who it was who fathered the child you're carrying?'

His cold sarcasm hurt her more than anything that

had ever happened to her in her entire life. She could
have handled anger, insults, even physical violence—
anything that sprang from powerful emotional trauma.
This icy sarcasm, almost amounting to cynical indifference, was worse than if he'd stabbed a rusty blade
into her heart.

What she had feared had happened. He had already
gone away from her emotionally, relegating the magic
of their lovemaking to mere having sex.

And he was waiting for her answer, his eyes dark
and bleak, his mouth tight against his teeth. She gathered up the last vestiges of her strength, exhaled a
shuddering sigh.

'Sam.'

CHAPTER TWO

HE STRODE away, his shoulders hard and high and rigid. Elena couldn't move. Her feet felt as if they'd been welded to the cool marble floor tiles, and her arms were wrapped tightly around her quivering body.

Only when she heard the sound of the car he'd hired to bring them from the airport was she shocked into movement. Her flying feet scattered rugs as she ran to the front of the house, tugging open the sturdy front door, racing through the courtyard and out onto the stony track.

He couldn't leave her like this, run out on her, with nothing said, nothing explained—never mind resolved! But the cloud of dust, the noise of the rapidly receding engine told her that he could. And had.

Her first instinct was to get her own car out of the barn and follow him. But he would hate that. Even if she caught up with him nothing would be achieved. He had taken what he obviously felt he needed; time alone to sort his head out.

If only he had given her enough time to explain, to tell him the whole truth. He would still be hurting... But not this much.

Pushing her fist against her teeth, to stop herself throwing her head back and howling her pain to the burning bowl of the sky, she ran to a rocky outcrop, uncaring of the sharp edges cutting into the soles of her bare feet, and watched until the cloud of dust disappeared on the valley floor. Then walked slowly back to the house, defeated, wretched.

Jed would come back in his own good time, and all she could do was wait. But for the first time ever she could find no comfort in her beautiful home, the symbol of her fabulous success. Lovingly recreated from what had been little more than a near derelict shell, her home, her gardens, her slice of Andalucian mountainside, had previously reinforced her belief in herself, in the financial and emotional independence she'd made for herself.

As she'd confided in Sam, on what had turned out to be his last night in Spain, 'When I left my husband ten years ago and came out to Cadiz, I had nothing—not even my self-respect, because Liam had taken that away. I worked in bars and lived in a miserable one-room flat and took to writing in what spare time I had as a way of forgetting. Luckily, it paid off, and what had begun as therapy became my whole existence.'

The wine had been flowing freely on that dark February evening, and she'd lighted a fire in the great stone-hooded hearth, because the evenings were chilly in the hills. Sam's mood had been strangely reflective, almost sombre, the atmosphere—that of long-standing easy friendship—conducive to soul-baring.

'And now, because my books took off in a big way, I have everything. A successful career and pride in my work, a beautiful home in a lovely part of the world, a wonderful circle of friends—more financial security than I ever dreamed of having. Everything except a child, and sometimes that hurts. I guess I hear my biological clock chiming out yet another passing hour. But as I have no intention of ever marrying again...'

She shrugged wryly, sipping her wine to deaden the ache of her empty womb, her empty arms. Liam had adamantly refused to contemplate fatherhood. He'd wanted a glamorous wife on his arm, not a worn-out rag of a woman, stuck at home tied to a bunch of grizzling kids.

'We have a lot in common, you and I.' Sam levered himself out of the comfy leather-upholstered armchair on the opposite side of the crackling log fire and opened the last of the three bottles of wine he'd brought when he'd invited himself for supper earlier. 'You want a child, but you can't stomach the idea of a husband to go with it—once badly bitten and all that.' He withdrew the cork with a satisfying plop, and although Elena knew she'd already had more than was wise, she allowed him to refill her glass.

Over the two years he'd been coming to this corner of Spain, to snatch a few days' relaxation between assignments for one of the more erudite broadsheets, he had become her dear friend. There was something driven about him that she could relate to, and nothing remotely sexual so she was doubly comfortable with him.

She smiled at him with affection. Too right, she didn't want or need a husband. Never again—the one she'd had had turned out to be a disaster.

Sam kicked a log back into place with a booted foot and stood staring into the flames, his glass loosely held in his hands. 'I'm dead against marriage, too, but for different reasons. With my dodgy lifestyle, it's not on. Besides—and I wouldn't admit this to just anyone— I've a fairly low sex drive. Unlike my brother.'

Jed. Sam often talked about him. He lived in the

family home, somewhere old and impressive in the shires, and headed the family business—gobbling up any opposition, sitting on a fat portfolio. And now, it appeared, he was a womaniser too.

But Sam was telling her, 'Since his late teens he's always had women making a play for him—nubile, dewy-eyed daughters of the landed gentry, women who lunch, tough career cookies, the lot. But, to give him his due, he's picky and very discreet. Mind you, he'll marry some day, to get an heir. He wouldn't want the family business to die out with him. But not me. All my emotional, mental and physical energies go into my job. I only feel properly alive when facing danger, grabbing photographs and copy from volatile situations.'

Elena hated it when he talked like that; it made her feel edgy. She watched him drain his glass, heard him say, 'Like you, the only regret I have is knowing how unlikely I am to ever have a child of my own. To my way of thinking, passing on one's genes is the only type of immortality any of us can ever hope for.' He turned to watch her then, his lean, wiry frame tense. 'There is an answer, though, for both of us. I'd be more than happy to offer myself as a donor. I can think of no other woman better to carry my child. I'd make no demands, other than the right to visit with you both when possible. Never interfere. Think about it.'

He put his empty glass on a side table and bent to kiss her lightly on the forehead. 'You would never have to lose your freedom and independence to a husband; you wouldn't have to go through the messy business of sleeping around to get the child you're beginning to crave. No risk of nasty diseases! And I'd get my single claim to immortality.' He smiled into her shell-shocked eyes. 'Sleep on it, why don't you? I'll call you in the morning. If you want to go for it, we can get straight back to London and start things moving. There's a private clinic headed by a professor of gynaecology who owes me a favour—it's useful, sometimes, to have friends in high places! Night, Elena—I'll let myself out.'

At first she'd dismissed his idea as utterly preposterous, but the longer she'd sat over the dying embers the more deeply she'd thought about it, and the less outlandish it had become.

He'd talked about her craving for a child, and he was right. Sometimes, the need to hold her own baby in her arms was an actual physical pain, a deep, regretful sorrow that wouldn't go away. And when that happened—with increasing regularity—everything she had achieved for herself seemed suddenly worthless.

She would never marry again, and the thought of sleeping around in order to get pregnant was deeply repugnant. And she liked and respected Sam Nolan, didn't she? Admired him. The child who carried his genes would be blessed.

When he called the following morning her answer was an affirmative.

She'd made the necessary trip to the London clinic with Sam, never once imagining that almost six weeks later she would be at his funeral. Deeply saddened by the loss of a talented young life to a stray sniper's bullet in a war-torn East African state, and more than devastated because only that morning after a month of hope, she'd discovered that his idea hadn't worked.

Sam hadn't achieved his claim to immortality and she would never have a child to hold and love.

She'd met Jed at that simple, heart-wrenching ceremony, and from that moment on everything had changed. For both of them.

It was dark when Jed finally returned. Elena, pacing the courtyard, heard the sound of the approaching car and panicked.

Would he view her pregnancy differently when he learned how the baby had been conceived? Would he believe she and his younger brother had never been lovers? Accept the fact that they had been merely good friends who'd found themselves in a similar frustrating situation and had gone for a rational solution?

The dim outside lights were on—soft golden light reflecting from the surrounding whitened stone walls of her sprawling home, tendrils of soft mist trailing gently around terracotta planters burgeoning with foliage and sweetly scented flowers.

The silence when the engine cut out was immense, the night air sultry. Perspiration beaded her face as she waited, tension tying her in knots. She had to make him listen to her, believe her. Surely their love for each other entitled her to a fair hearing?

He appeared at last in the arched doorway to the courtyard, his big body taut, very still. The softly diffused lights, black shadows and trails of mist made him look desperately forbidding. Elena grasped the back of one of the cast-iron two-seaters that flanked the outdoor table. Her spine felt as if it had turned to water; she needed some support.

'Where were you?' she asked thickly as the minutes

of fraught silence ticked away. He didn't appear to be in any hurry to break the ice. Someone had to do it.

'Seville.' The short answer was clipped. But at least he began to walk over the cobbles towards her. 'As you know, Nolan's are to acquire a retail outlet in Seville. I was due to meet our architect in a fortnight's time, to decide which of two suitable properties to go for.' He stopped, feet away from her, almost as if, she thought hysterically, the air surrounding her might contaminate him. 'For reasons I'm sure you'll understand, I thought today might be as good as any to get back in harness.'

Elena flinched. They'd planned on a three-week honeymoon, here at her home, Las Rocas, then to spend a week in Seville together to meet with the architect and explore the lovely city. Plainly, the honeymoon was over. But after her bombshell what else could she have expected?

She made a small, one-handed gesture towards him, her throat thick with sudden tears. But if he noticed the way she reached out to him he didn't respond, and she let her hand drop defeatedly back to her side and said raggedly, 'Can we talk?'

'Of course.' The dip of his head was coldly polite. 'But inside. It's been a long day.'

He moved towards the house and Elena followed, pushing her long straight hair back from her face with a decidedly shaky hand. She could have borne his rage, his recriminations, far more easily. At least then she would have known what was going on inside his head, could have reassured him, told it as it was, asked him to try to understand.

She hadn't met him, much less fallen in love with

him, when she'd made the decision to be artificially impregnated—for reasons that had seemed right and sane and reasonable then. He was an intelligent, compassionate man. Surely he would understand how she had felt at the time?

Striding straight to the kitchen, Jed reached for the bottle of Scotch tucked away in one of the cupboards, unscrewed the cap and poured a more than generous measure for himself.

'In view of your condition, I won't ask you to join me.' He swallowed half the golden liquid, then pulled a chair away from the chunky pine table and sat, long legs outstretched, the fingertips of one hand drumming against the grainy wooden top, his dark head tilted slightly in insolent enquiry. 'So talk. I'm listening. Or would you rather I set the conversational ball rolling?'

His voice was so cold, almost as cold as his eyes. They reached deep inside her and froze her soul. Shakily she pulled a chair out for herself and sat on the edge, not opposite him, but further down the table so he would have to turn to look at her.

He didn't, and she was as glad as she could be under these impossibly hateful circumstances. She didn't want to see the frozen indifference of his eyes, not when they had once looked at her with so much love.

She shuddered suddenly, convulsively, knotting her hands together in her lap. Briefly, her eyes flicked round the farmhouse kitchen—heavy copper pans gleaming against the white-painted stone walls, the great stone chimney breast, gleaming terracotta floor tiles and carved, polished wood dressers, the pots of scented geraniums on the broad windowsills.

She'd always loved this room, and this last week,

in Pilar's absence, she and Jed had made their meals here together. Chopping vegetables and fresh herbs from the garden, washing fruit. Talking, laughing together, sometimes catching each other's eyes, understanding the need, the love, reaching for each other, the meal in the making forgotten...

It didn't seem possible that all the love and laughter, that magical feeling of closeness had gone. She wouldn't let herself even think that it would never come back. Yet his attitude had erected a mountain between them. She didn't know if she was strong enough to climb it.

She had to try, though. It was imperative. She flicked her tongue over her dry lips as she struggled to find the words. The right words. Words that would help him understand. But he said impatiently, 'As you seem to have been struck dumb, I'll do the talking.' He swallowed what was left of his whisky and swung round on his chair, looking at her now from narrowed, unforgiving eyes. 'I've thought about our distasteful situation and reached certain non-negotiable decisions. We stay married,' he stated grimly, then reached for the bottle and poured another shot into his glass.

Something tore at Elena's heart, a savage little pain. 'You considered divorce?' After what they'd been to each other she could hardly believe it. Would he hate himself for even thinking about it once he knew the truth? Would she be able to forget how he'd considered cutting her right out of his life without giving her the opportunity to explain herself?

'Naturally. What else did you expect?' He wasn't looking at her now, but staring at his glass as he twisted it around between his fingers, watching the way the liquid caught the light and fractured it. 'Under the circumstances it was the first thing I thought of. However, for two reasons, I decided against it. The first Catherine, my mother. She likes you.' The very tone of his voice told her he couldn't now imagine why. 'Our marriage was the only thing that lightened her grief over Sam's death. A divorce, so soon, would be rather more than she could be expected to bear.

'The second reason for keeping the marriage going is my brother's unborn child. I don't blame Sam for any of this. He died without knowing he'd made you pregnant. So, for my brother's sake, we stay married. I intend to take a full part in his child's upbringing. Call it a duty of care. Sam tended to mock me for being the dutiful son, but perhaps, wherever he is, he'll be thankful for it now.'

For a moment his eyes were drenched with the pain of grief, and Elena's heart bled for him. She wanted to reach out to him, to comfort him, to tell him that everything could be all right if he'd let it be, if he'd listen to her and try to understand.

She was halfway out of her seat, on her way to him, but the quelling darkness of his expression put her back again, his voice cutting as he told her, 'We will put up a good front, for the sake of my mother and the child when he or she arrives. But, that apart, I want as little as possible to do with you. We'll return to the UK in three weeks' time, as arranged, and I'll get out of your hair as much as I can—visit the overseas branches. You can make the excuse that travelling doesn't agree with pregnancy.'

He pushed away from the table and rinsed his glass

out at the deep stone sink, upturning it on the drainer, and Elena choked back a sob.

Every word he'd uttered had strengthened the wall between them, making it impossible to breach. Whatever she said to him now, whether he believed her or not, those words—the brutal ending of their marriage in all but name—would never be forgotten.

'And if I don't agree to this—this farce!' She struggled to her feet, but had to support herself against the table. 'I want you to listen to my point of view. I want you to hear what really happened. I have that right.'

'You have no rights!' He flung down the towel he'd been drying his hands on, the first sign of a real emotion directed at her since his return showing through. 'And you brought this "farce" on yourself. You married me while knowing you could be pregnant by my brother,' he castigated harshly. 'Why? Because you didn't fancy single parenthood? One brother was lost to you so you might as well settle on the other? He might not live such a dangerously fascinating, swashbuckling type of life, might not be as pretty to look at, but he'd do? Marry me and hope fantastic sex would make me overlook everything else.'

He turned away, as if he couldn't bear to look at her. 'Well, you were wrong. It didn't. You're good in bed, I'll give you that. But not that good. In any case, I can get fantastic sex whenever I want. No strings, no messy secrets, no regrets.'

That hurt. If he'd ripped her heart out of her body with his bare hands it couldn't have hurt more.

Pain took her by the throat and shook her, making speech impossible. But she had, somehow, to make him understand, to begin the process of partially exonerating herself, for both their sakes. Distrust of her was turning him into a man she didn't know.

'When we first met, I truly believed…' Her voice, difficult to push past the constriction in her throat, faltered and died as she remembered the way he'd approached her after the graveside ceremony. 'You must be Elena Keele; Sam often spoke about you. Don't go away.' He had touched her black-gloved hand briefly, and warmth had momentarily displaced the aching sorrow in his eyes. 'Come back to the house. I think your company would be a comfort to my mother. And to me. Through Sam, I already feel I know you.'

And so it had begun.

Aware that he was watching her struggle for words, the straight line of his mouth twisted to one side, sardonically interested in her fumbling attempts to excuse the inexcusable, she went scarlet and told him roughly, 'I thought I wasn't pregnant. I started a period on the morning of Sam's funeral.' It had been sketchy, and of very short duration, but she'd put that down to the shock of learning of her friend's death, the rush to get a flight to London, hire a car and drive out to his home village to pay her last respects.

The next had been equally slight, but it hadn't crossed her mind that she might be carrying Sam's child. She'd been back in Spain for two weeks then, regretfully leaving Jed in England. They'd spent two weeks getting to know each other, learning to accept the unbelievable fact of love at first sight. But she'd had a deadline to meet, and if they were to be married as soon as possible—which they had both known almost from that first moment of meeting—Jed had a lot of business ends to tie up, too.

The love, the magic, the precious feeling of being born for each other couldn't have disappeared so completely. Surely it couldn't?

She approached him with more determination. He had to hear her out. 'Jed—Sam and I—'

'Spare me!' he cut across her, his eyes derisive. 'I don't want to hear the sordid details.' He headed for the door, his footsteps ringing firmly on the tiled floor. 'And I'm sure you'll understand if I don't believe a word you say. Why keep a testing kit around if you were so certain your affair with my brother hadn't left you with any music to face? Why use it at all?'

'Because I'd begun to feel nauseous in the morning! I believed pregnancy was out of the question, but did the test just to make doubly sure!' she shot back at him, her temper rising. How could a man who'd said he'd love her till the day he died refuse to properly hear her side of the story, refuse point-blank to believe a word she said?

Her shoulders rigid, she bunched her hands into fists at her sides and told him, her voice grinding out the slow words, 'Sam and I were *never* lovers.'

'No? One-night stand, was it? Don't try to tell me he forced himself on you. Sam wasn't like that. It was more likely to be the other way around. From my experience during this last week your appetite for sex is pretty well insatiable.'

Bitterness was stamped all over his harsh features, and it held his spine in a rigid line as he walked out of the room. In that moment she hated him.

She had never hated anyone before, not even Liam. She had despised him, but never hated him. The savage emotion consumed her. She paced the terracotta tiles, her arms wrapped around her slender body, holding herself together in case she should explode with the hot rage that flared and flamed inside her.

How dared he treat her as if she were trash? Accuse her of such monstrous things? And where had the man she loved more than her life disappeared to? Had he ever really existed, or had he been mere wish-fulfilment, a figment of her imagination? The man who had just walked out on her was a cold-hearted, arrogant, egotistical monster!

He could forget his 'non-negotiable' decision of a sham marriage. She would accept no part of it. Did he think he had a God-given right to dish out orders, arrogantly decide how she would live out the rest of her life?

Did he really think she would stay legally tied to a man who thought so badly of her? Did he imagine, for one moment, that she'd unquestioningly suffer the misery such a vile arrangement would bring her?

As far as she was concerned their marriage was over in every way there was. She had no intention of returning to England with him, living a lie. She was perfectly capable of looking after her child on her own—that had been the original intention, after all.

Her child did not need a father figure, especially one as all-fired intransigent, bloody-minded and arrogant as Jed Nolan!

First thing in the morning she would tell him to pack his bags, get out of her home. She never wanted to have to see him again.

CHAPTER THREE

SHE didn't get the opportunity to ask him to leave. He'd already done it.

The sun had only just begun to gild the flanks of the rugged hills with new-day light when she left her solitary bed and dragged herself downstairs after a monumentally miserable and sleepless night.

Which bedroom Jed had used she had no idea, and didn't care, she told herself as she secured the belt of the robe she'd thrown on more tightly around her narrow waist. As soon as he surfaced she would ask him to leave, announce that she'd be in touch, through her solicitor, some time in the future. Let him know that he wasn't the only one who could make decisions and hurl them around like concrete slabs.

If he wasn't prepared to listen to her, to believe her, then their relationship wasn't worth keeping—certainly not the acrimonious, desolately empty relationship he had in mind. Better by far to make a clean break.

Making for the kitchen for the coffee she suddenly dramatically needed, she saw his note the moment she pushed open the door. A scrap of paper on the polished pine table top. It didn't say a lot, just a scrawl of distinctive black handwriting. 'I'll be in Seville for the next three weeks. I'll collect you for our return journey.'

The hell you will! Elena scrunched the paper up and

hurled it at the wall. Frustrated by his disappearance, before she could tell him she had no intention of meekly tugging her forelock and submitting to his orders, she felt her blood pressure hit the roof.

She didn't even know which hotel he'd be using in Seville. She couldn't get in touch and remind him that she was perfectly capable of making the decisions that would affect the rest of her life, that no way would she be returning to England, simpering and smiling and pretending to be deliriously happy. No way!

Hot tears flooded her eyes. Had she been secretly hoping that Jed would have come to his senses this morning, found enough trust in her to believe her story? If so, she'd been a fool. Well, no more.

She'd just have to sit out the next three weeks with the rage festering away inside her, and— Suddenly the now all too familiar morning sickness struck, and twenty wretched minutes later she was standing under a warm shower, patting her still flat tummy and murmuring wryly, 'You're certainly giving Mummy a hard time, Troublebunch!'

Even as the tender smile curved her lips her eyes filled with tears again. Tears for Sam, who would never know he'd left a child behind, for herself, and for Jed, who had lost something wonderful that could never be retrieved.

Warm needles of water washed the tears away, and she dried herself, wrapped her long hair in a towel, dressed in cotton shorts and a halter-neck top and told herself they were the last tears she would shed for any of them.

Life went on.

She had her child to look forward to, and she would

love it to distraction and give him or her the happiest life any child could want. Now that she was marginally calmer she could see that, in a way, it was a blessing that Jed had taken off. That action alone told her that he'd never truly loved her. If he had, he'd have trusted her, believed her, asked for more details. It had also saved her from a demeaning slanging match, from allowing all her hurt to pour out and hit him right between the eyes.

When she next saw Jed she would be able to tell him of her own decisions, calmly and rationally. She was intelligent enough to know that no amount of rage could alter anything. He despised her now; all the love had gone and nothing she could do or say would bring it back. That was a fact. Hard to face, but not impossible.

She could handle the hurt; she'd managed before and would manage again. Certainly the way Liam had hurt her had been a mere pinprick compared to this. But then she'd had nothing, just a mother who'd wrung her hands and wailed, prophesied heaven alone knew what horrors if she insisted on skipping the country with little more than the clothes she stood up in.

But from having nothing and no one she'd made a good life for herself. At least this time round she had a successful career to fall back on, and was carrying the child she'd begun to need so desperately.

So, on the whole, she reasoned, wondering if she could manage a glass of water and a slice of dry toast without upsetting her unborn baby, everything balanced out and she could hack it.

She wasn't at all sure about that one week later, when Jed arrived with his mother.

She hadn't been able to think about starting a new book, and hadn't responded to the faxes from her agent which had come chattering through over the last couple of days—apologising for interrupting her honeymoon, but apparently excited over some awards ceremony to be held in London. She hadn't been interested. One day she'd have to read through them properly, absorb what her agent was trying to tell her and respond. But not now. Not yet.

She'd driven down to the village and told Pilar to take two more weeks' leave, and then had sought the solitude she so desperately needed in the hot few acres of Spanish earth that was her garden.

She was weeding amongst the massed clumps of sweet-smelling carnations that bordered one of the twisting paved paths when she heard the car. Brushing her hands down the sides of her cotton skirt, she stood up and walked towards the house, resenting the intrusion. Resenting it to the point of internal explosion when she saw Jed handing his mother from the car.

She couldn't imagine what either of them was doing here, or what she could possibly say to them—especially Catherine Nolan, who was one of the nicest women to draw breath.

Wearing a pale blue linen suit, the older woman looked less stressed out than the grieving mother she'd come to know during the two weeks she'd stayed in Netherhaye, the family home in rural Hertfordshire. Though she had perked up enormously for the quiet wedding, bossing the caterers and florists around, mak-

ing sure the small reception back at Netherhaye was
as perfect as it could possibly be.

'Elena!' Catherine beamed as she became aware of
her daughter-in-law's approach. 'How good of you to
agree to let me come—only for a few days, I promise.
I won't intrude longer than that!'

So Jed hadn't told his mother of the complications
that had rendered their marriage null and void.
Catherine wouldn't be looking like a plump, slightly
flustered, happy mother hen if he had. But then he
wouldn't, of course, she reminded herself, doing her
best to find a smile of sorts. Hadn't duping his parent
into believing everything was blissful been one of his
two main priorities?

'It's lovely to see you.' She bent to receive
Catherine's kiss and didn't look at Jed. He was re-
moving luggage from the boot, just a shadowy presence in the background, and that was the way he had
to stay if she was to hold onto her sanity, swallow
back the scalding renewal of the pain and rage she'd
talked herself into believing was over and done with.
'I'm sure you're ready for a drink.'

'Oh, I'd love one. It's quite a drive from Jerez airport, isn't it? But such lovely countryside—oh, what
a gorgeous courtyard—all those lilies! And will you
just look at those geraniums? They never get that huge
at home!'

Barely hearing the spate of compliments on her
home, Elena led the older woman into the cool, airy
sitting room and watched her plop down into a deep
comfy armchair with an audible sigh of relief.

'Bliss! Now I can take my shoes off.'

'And I can fetch you that drink.'

Elena escaped into the kitchen. She saw Jed toting luggage up the stairs, clenched her jaw and ignored him, closing the kitchen door behind her firmly. She could have gone after him and demanded to know what the hell he thought he was doing, bringing his mother here when their marriage, so recently begun, was well and truly over, leading the poor deluded woman to believe that she, Elena, had agreed to this visit.

But she didn't. She simply wanted to hide. During the past week she had talked herself into believing she could handle the irretrievable shocking breakdown, that when she saw him again it wouldn't hurt because sensibly, being an intelligent adult and not a soppy child, and because she'd done it once before, she knew how to cut her losses and go on.

But it did hurt. It hurt like hell.

She reached for two wine glasses and a bottle of white Rioja from the fridge; she needed the stiffening, even if Catherine didn't.

Catherine did. 'How deliciously cold. It hits the spot! Isn't Jed joining us?'

'He's taking your cases up.' And taking an inordinate amount of time about it, she thought edgily, doing her best to sound relaxed—though why should she bother, when Catherine would learn, sooner rather than later, that her new daughter-in-law was shortly to become an ex?

While Catherine chattered about her flight out, Elena, wine in hand, perched on the arm of one of the chairs and wondered whether to break the news now. Catherine would have to know, because following Jed's orders and pretending the marriage was fine when it wasn't was something she was not prepared to do.

She was trying to decide whether she should dress it up some way, and how, or whether she should come straight out with it when Catherine stopped her thought processes stone-dead.

'I have to tell you—your marriage to my son was one of the happiest occasions of my life, Elena. It didn't make up for losing Sam, nothing could ever do that, but it helped enormously—helped ease the dreadful grief and gave me something good to think about. Since I lost their father, all I've ever wanted is happiness for my boys.'

She looked so earnest, her eyes rather too moist, tears not far away, because she was still trying to come to terms with the worst thing that could happen to a woman: the loss of her child. Elena felt her stomach give a sickening lurch. She didn't want to hear any more, but short of walking out of the room she couldn't avoid it.

'Like any mother, I wanted my boys settled with a good woman, happily married with children of their own. I'd begun to despair of it ever happening.' She gave Elena a soft, shaky smile. 'Sam—well, he was like a will o' the wisp, impossible to pin down or keep in a settled place, and Jed—well, he was too settled, too much a workaholic bachelor, wedded to the business. But when Jed invited you to stay at Netherhaye, after the funeral, it was like a blessing. Just to watch the two of you gave me joy—and hope for the future. I could see what had happened, any fool could. I watched the pair of you holding your feelings back— not only because to hurl yourselves into each other's arms might have seemed crass, in view of the circumstances, but because you were obviously making sure you got to know each other before you made any commitment. Though of course Jed and I already felt we knew you very well, through what Sam had told us.

'Knowing that my one remaining son had found the perfect love at last was the only thing that kept me going through those dark days. So when he phoned a few days ago, to check I was all right on my own, I asked if I could come on a short visit. I hadn't meant to,' she said earnestly, 'it just came out. I know you're on your honeymoon, but I suppose I needed to see you both to restore my faith in God, to remind myself He can dish out the good as well as the hard to bear.'

Her smile was now so loving and peaceful it made Elena's heart bleed. How could she spill out the truth and ruin this good woman's precarious contentment? Plunge her back into the dark abyss of grief where there was no glimmer of consolation to be found?

Jed had decided on the pretence of marital bliss because he had known what the truth would do to his grieving parent, and Elena could understand that, sympathise. His harsh dictates, so coldly spelled out for her, became more the reasoned decisions of a man who knew his duty.

He would hate the idea of putting on a front as much as she did, but felt, because of the tragic circumstances, that it was the only right thing to do.

She didn't want to understand, and heaven knew she didn't want to sympathise. She wanted to cut Jed right out of her life, never see or hear of him again, carry on with the long haul of forgetting the pain, the terrible slicing pain of seeing his precious love turn to hatred.

Not knowing what to say, she refilled Catherine's glass and took a gulp of her own as yet untouched wine, and Jed said from the doorway, 'Should you be drinking that?'

The sound of that cool voice with undertones of condemnation made her heart clench, especially when the penny dropped and she realised why he had asked that question. Alcohol and pregnancy didn't mix. Sam's baby was another of his priorities, another duty of care.

'Don't be so stuffy! It's almost suppertime. We're not hitting the sauce before breakfast! Come and join us.' Not knowing his reason for the criticism, Catherine turned to her son, raising her glass, proud maternal love in her eyes.

Putting her own glass down on a side table, aware that her hands were shaking, that every darn thing in-side her was shaking, Elena risked an under-lash look at her husband.

He sauntered casually into the room, with a smile for his mother, hands stuffed into the pockets of his close-fitting dark trousers, the silk of his white shirt falling in fluid folds from his wide shoulders.

Yet there was strain there, there in the deepening of the lines that bracketed his beautiful, passionate male mouth, the tell-tale pallor beneath the olive tones of his skin. The past week had been tough on him, too.

But it was all entirely his own fault. She quelled the momentary surge of compassion. If he had given her the basic human right of being heard. If he'd given her the opportunity to tell him about the clinic treat-ment then he would have believed her when she'd told him that she and Sam had never been lovers.

'Now, you two…' Catherine beamed at them both indiscriminately, and Elena wondered if her mother-in-law was so blinded by what she wanted to believe that she couldn't sense something was wrong. 'I didn't invite myself here just to play gooseberry. There's something I need to discuss with you both. I could have said it on the phone, or written, but I wanted to see you…'

As the older woman's voice trailed uncertainly away Elena knew her present contentment was a fragile thing, with dark grief lurking beneath the surface of her courage, waiting for the opportunity to reclaim her.

'We're delighted you came,' Jed put in swiftly, briefly squeezing his mother's plump shoulder as he walked past to stand by Elena. 'We haven't done any sightseeing at all, so your being here gives us the ideal opportunity—we can do it together. I know Elena's anxious to show us her favourite places.'

Elena knew no such thing! Playing the devoted ecstatic wife for an audience of one while they trotted round the countryside would kill her! And when Jed went on to ask, 'So, what was it you wanted to discuss, Ma?' Elena shot to her feet and grabbed the first excuse to get out of there she could find.

'It's time I made a start on supper. You must be hungry, Catherine. You can tell us what's on your mind while we eat.'

She took her wine and fled, closing the kitchen door behind her, her heart punching against her breastbone. Catherine had mentioned staying a few days. Not long. But it would be purgatory. How could she pretend she and Jed were devoted newlyweds? Yet how could she do anything other? She couldn't heap more misery on that poor woman's head!

She and Jed would have to find a way out. She didn't know how, but she'd come up with something. She'd have to. The present situation couldn't be borne.

Tiredly, she carried her glass to the sink and tipped the wine away. Jed had been right, of course. Pregnancy and alcohol didn't mix.

His cool voice slid over her. 'I'm glad you agree I'm right.' He took the empty glass from her nerveless fingers and watched the last of the wine drain away.

Elena shuddered. She hadn't heard him follow her, and the coldness of his voice made her feel as if a wave of icy water had washed over her. How could he have forgotten everything they'd been to each other so completely and so callously?

Yet hadn't she, over this last endless week, been trying to do the same?

It was probably the only way, she conceded now, and turned away from him. 'Of course you were right. But you're not always, and you'd do well to remember that.' And he could ponder that, or not, as he chose. He had refused to hear her side of the story, walked all over her attempts to explain. She wasn't going to put herself in the position of being humiliated all over again. 'Why don't you go and entertain Catherine? Leave me to make supper.'

There were things she needed to say to him, but they would have to wait. Right now she wanted him and his icy voice and his tight-boned face well away from where she was. Her emotions had been in a mess ever since she'd discovered she was pregnant, and his return—with Catherine—had sent them skittering around, completely out of control.

She couldn't handle it, and didn't even want to have to try.

But Jed had other ideas. 'She's on the patio, soaking up the sun and the rest of the wine. She's not as young as she was and travelling tires her.'

'Then she shouldn't have come!' Elena bit out as she swung round to face him. 'What do you think I felt like when I saw you arriving together? The least you could have done was phone and warn me!' The moment the words were out she wished she could swallow them back. The poor woman had only made the journey to reassure herself, remind herself that there were things to be happy about. This situation with Jed had got her so she didn't know what she was saying or thinking.

'I didn't know you were so selfish.' Cold eyes raked her with glittering dislike. 'But then there were other things you made sure I didn't know.' His mouth twisted bitterly, his eyes continuing a brutal assessment. 'You look a mess. Freshen up while I make a meal. And behave yourself in front of Catherine. If you upset her I'll make you wish you'd never been born.'

Elena stalked out before she exploded. By the time she reached the relative sanctuary of her room her heart felt big enough to belong to an elephant, big enough to burst. How dared he treat her as if she were scum? How dared he?

She kicked her shoes into a corner, dragged the faded old cotton skirt and gardening shirt from her quivering body and stamped into the bathroom. Ten minutes later, wrapped in a towel, she knew what she had to do. For her unborn child's sake she had to stay calm. And to have any hope of achieving that she had to be careful not to sink to Jed's level, not to say vile and hurtful things, and not—most definitely not—rant and rave and throw things!

She chose a fitted silk sheath that ended a couple of inches above her knees and left her lightly tanned arms bare. The colour matched her eyes and the fabric clung to every curve. Soon now she'd start to bulge, and have to wear tents, and after the birth she'd probably turn matronly—so if she wanted to look on the cool side of sexy while she still could, who was there to stop her? Certainly not her pig of a husband.

To counteract the sexy length of leg on view, the way the silk of her dress lovingly caressed the curve of breast, tummy and thigh, she pulled her hair back from her face in a elegant upswept style and touched her wrists with old-fashioned lavender water.

Cool and sexy, both. And if the enigma annoyed the man she wished she'd been sensible enough not to fall in love with, tough.

'My goodness—you do look lovely!' Catherine said as Elena joined her on the patio, where Jed was putting a selection of salads down on the table.

'Thank you.' Elena managed a smile as she sank into the padded seat next to her mother-in-law. She knew Jed had turned from what he'd been doing to look at her, but refused to meet his eyes. She'd been on the receiving end of too many contemptuous looks coming from him to go looking for more.

'Believe it or not, I used to have a shape! Then the boys arrived, and that was that!' Catherine's eyes twinkled at her, and Elena thought, My God, one day she's going to have to know she's going to be a grand-mother. Sam's child.

She pressed the tips of her fingers to her temples. How would the older woman take the news? It seemed that every time she took a breath another problem popped up. The decision she and poor dead Sam had taken was creating unbelievable ripples—

'I nodded off for a few minutes, I'm afraid, what with the sun and the wine and the worry of flying on my own for the very first time,' Catherine was con-fessing, unaware of Elena's boiling thoughts. 'Or I would have changed for supper. Should I trot along and tidy up now?'

'No.' She didn't want to be left alone with Jed. She still felt too raw to cope with any more of his hurtful comments. He'd disappeared back into the kitchen, but he could be back at any moment. The negative had come out too quickly, too harshly. Making a conscious effort, Elena smiled. 'You're fine as you are, really. I'd much prefer you to stay and chat!'

And chat she did, and was still at it when Jed finally appeared with a dish of pasta dressed with olive oil and garlic. 'We seem to be running low on provisions,' he commented mildly, not making it sound like a crit-icism for his mother's benefit. 'So we'll make do with pasta and salads, OK?'

It would have to be. Elena hadn't bothered to shop, hadn't felt like eating during the last nightmare week, and his lumping them together, making them a 'we' made her disproportionally annoyed.

'Scandalous, isn't it, Catherine?' Her smile was as cool as the way she was wearing her hair, as cool as her cologne. 'We couldn't bring ourselves to venture out into the real world, even for food.'

She did look at Jed then, saw that her taunt had rubbed salt into an open wound, watched his mouth tighten, his jaw clench, saw raw pain in his eyes and told herself she didn't care. He could dish out hurt but he couldn't take it. At least he *could* take it, she amended as she watched him hand dishes to Catherine, but he sure as hell didn't like it.

'Well, now,' his mother commented comfortably, blissfully unaware of undertones. 'That discussion I told you I needed.' She dabbed olive oil from her mouth with a soft paper napkin. 'As you know, Elena, your mother helped me organise your wedding reception, and I persuaded her to stay with me at Netherhaye while you were working back here before the wedding and Jed was tying up loose ends, as he called it, all over the place. And, to cut a long story short, we grew very friendly in a very short space of time. Now...' She glanced at her son. 'I don't know whether I'm jumping the gun, but I rather hope you two will make Netherhaye your home, bring up your children there as your father and I did. It's been in the family such a very long time.'

Elena caught the warning glint of steel in Jed's smoky eyes and bit down hard on her lower lip, dragging it back between her teeth, holding back a cry of denial as Catherine went on, 'I certainly don't want to rattle around there on my own, and, despite intruding on you here for a few days, I'm of the opinion that newly weds don't want to find a parent lurking around every corner, cramping their style. So, either way, I'll be moving to somewhere very much smaller.'

Elena registered Jed's harsh inhalation and wondered if he was inwardly applauding his mother's decision. It would make things easier for him, wouldn't it? They wouldn't have to play at happy couples very often; he could trot her out on social occasions then pop her back in her box and forget all about her.

Over her dead body!

'Are you sure about that, Ma?' Jed asked, leaning forward slightly, the better to judge his parent's true feelings in the dwindling evening light. 'I don't want you to think you have to make a snap decision, or that Elena and I wouldn't be happy to have you live with us.'

Elena watched him narrowly. He looked and sounded totally sincere. On the one hand, having his mother remove herself from their immediate orbit would make life a lot easier for him. But, on the other, he was deeply fond of Catherine, cared about her. The whole idea of pretending their marriage was normal had stemmed from his desire to keep the older woman happily deluded, spare her any further grief.

'You know how you love the old place; all your memories are there—and you're besotted by your garden!'

'And having seen something of Elena's, and her beautiful home, I know Netherhaye will be in good hands.' Catherine smiled gently and put her hand over her son's. 'Sam's gone now, and in any case he wouldn't have wanted the responsibility. Netherhaye is yours.'

'Even so,' Jed said gruffly, 'I don't like to think of your being on your own. Not yet, not until...' His voice tailed off, and despite herself Elena had to admire his understanding and compassion. If only he had extended a tenth of it in her direction!

'You really mustn't worry about me!' Catherine smiled at both of them. 'What I was about to tell you is I won't be alone! I can't remember who got the idea first, but Susan and I are going to set up home together. There's a cottage for sale in the village—you remember the Fletchers, Jed? Well, they're moving to the south coast, to be nearer their married daughter and grandchildren, and while I'm here breaking the news Susan is doing the business with the agent and putting her own home up for sale. There! What do you think of that?'

Elena didn't know what to think. Jed was saying something, but her head was buzzing so loudly she couldn't hear a word. Her mother hadn't mentioned anything about selling the small house in Birmingham where Elena had been born. The fact that she hadn't taken her into her confidence hurt.

'As soon as this house was habitable, I asked her to live with me,' Elena stated numbly. 'She said she was too long in the tooth to uproot herself. Several years on, she's obviously changed her mind.'

She pulled herself to her feet. The stars were bright now, in the dark velvet sky, and the scent of mountain herbs was released in the soft warm breeze. She couldn't stand it, any of it! The night was so beautiful while her emotions were so painful, twisted and ugly. 'If you'll excuse me, Catherine, I'll clear away.' She balanced dishes and plates one on top of another and forced a thin smile. 'Ask Jed if you need anything.'

'Did you have to be so bloody curt?'
The bedroom door closed quietly behind him and

Elena pulled the soft linen sheet up to her chin, swallowing the hot hard lump in her throat.

Contempt blazed from his narrowed eyes and she really couldn't taken any more.

Her mother had never forgiven her for the failure of her marriage to Liam. She had thought the sun rose with her handsome young son-in-law. Even when she'd learned the truth she had tentatively suggested, 'Perhaps you drove him to it, dear?'

Her own marriage had been a miserable thing. Elena's father had had one affair after another, finally disappearing off the scene altogether when Elena was fifteen. Naturally Susan had wanted her only child's marriage to be perfect. She would be even more unforgiving now, when she learned that her second attempt at matrimonial happy-ever-after had been even less successful than the first!

'Go away,' she said wearily. 'I'm in no mood to talk right now.' Though there were things that needed to be said, of course there were—decisions of her own he had to hear about. And she had to make another attempt to break through his stubborn refusal to listen to her story. She should have told him about the treatment she'd undergone as soon as they'd realised they were falling in love. But Sam's death had been so recent, and Jed's grief so raw—a grief she hadn't wanted to exacerbate. She had decided it would be better to wait. And the treatment had been a failure— or so she'd truly believed at the time. She deeply regretted her decision to wait until time had softened the edges of Jed's grief.

Yes, there were things that had to be said, but the

stress and trauma of the past week had finally caught up with her, draining her of every last ounce of energy.

'You're "in no mood"—that figures.' He advanced slowly, unbuttoning his shirt. 'Your ego's too big to see round, isn't it? *Your* needs are the only things that matter. You agree to marry me, conveniently forgetting to mention that you and Sam were lovers, that there was a distinct possibility you might be carrying his child, then get all hurt and bewildered when I understandably say I want out.'

He pulled his shirt from the waistband of his trousers, the tanned skin of his tautly muscled torso gleaming in the soft diffused light, the line of his mouth condemning as he continued, 'And then you blank Catherine—who doesn't deserve it—because, *amazingly*,' he stressed insultingly, 'your own mother appears to prefer her company to yours.'

Elena closed her eyes, fighting to hold back a feeble sob. Never before had she felt this useless, unable to take one more brickbat. She had been barely nineteen when Liam Forrester—he of the sharp suits, fast cars and dazzling smile—had swept her off her feet. And only a year later her world had come crashing down when she'd discovered she was married to a common criminal. But she'd picked herself up, because she was basically a fighter, and made a new life for herself from the ashes of the old.

But now, it seemed, she'd lost it. Lost the ability to pick herself up and carry on and—'What are you doing?' she asked thickly, her eyes opening wide as the rustle of clothing sounded ominously close.

'What do you think?' His trousers joined his discarded shirt on the carved blanket box at the foot of the bed. Naked, apart from brief boxer shorts, his male magnificence made her throat clench.

'You can't sleep here!' She panicked, despising herself for not being able to invest the words with more authority. 'Our marriage, for what it was worth, is over.'

'So it is,' he agreed coolly. 'But don't worry, I've no intention of making demands on the delectable body you went to so much trouble to display this evening. What were you trying to do? Remind me of what I was missing? If so, it didn't work. Move over.'

'No.' She kept her eyes firmly closed as he removed his shorts, hugging the sheet more tightly under her chin because she was naked, too. And she hadn't done her best to look sexy to remind him. Or had she?

She felt the mattress dip and began to shake. Having him share her bed would be sheer, unmitigated torture.

'I'm not overjoyed about this, either,' he admitted drily as he extinguished the bedside light. 'But Catherine's always been an early riser. Crack of dawn and she's up and doing.' She felt him slide his legs beneath the sheet, punch the pillow. 'If she sees us coming from separate rooms in the morning she'll know something's wrong.'

'And that's all that matters, is it?' Elena snapped, stung. Didn't he consider her feelings at all?

'At the moment, yes,' he said, his voice cleaving the soft warm darkness. 'She's going through a tough time at the moment; I won't add to it. Sam was always head and shoulders her favourite. Naturally she wouldn't have wanted to lose either one of us. But she did, and I'm the one that's left. I feel guilty enough about that without adding to her grief. Just go to sleep, will you?'

He turned his back on her, carefully leaving a yawning space between them, and Elena lay rigidly, staring into the darkness.

What he'd said about feeling guilty was crazy. Wasn't it? Or was there something about his relationship with his brother that she didn't know about? Something that might explain the brutal transformation from a warm and loving husband, partner, friend and companion, the soul-mate she'd believed him to be, into a hard, uncaring, bitter adversary?

She didn't know, and if she asked he wouldn't tell her. He had refused to believe her when she'd truthfully said that she and Sam had never made love, closed his mind when she'd tried to explain, cut her out of his life and his heart.

Whatever it was that had troubled his relationship with Sam had risen up and cut out his love for her as surely and completely as a surgeon expertly wielding a very sharp knife.

CHAPTER FOUR

THE smooth rhythm of his breathing agitated her beyond bearing, set every nerve-end tingling. Lying as far from him as she could get, practically on the edge of the big double bed, she held her body stiffly, every muscle aching with tension.

How could he instantly fall into a healing, untroubled sleep? she thought resentfully. Why couldn't she? Why was she the one to lie awake, body aching, mind burning, every inch of her flesh craving his?

Why couldn't she write him off and calmly get on with her life as he obviously had?

If he'd truly loved her he'd have listened to her, trusted her. But he hadn't. He hadn't even loved her enough to do her the courtesy of at least listening to her explanations of what had happened between her and Sam. So why couldn't she stop loving him?

Unanswerable questions made jagged circuits of her brain, tormenting her, but just as she decided she'd be better off downstairs in her study, reading through those neglected faxes from her agent, she slid abruptly into exhausted sleep, and woke to find herself cuddled into Jed's naked body.

Hardly daring to breathe, Elena gingerly opened her eyes. Grey pre-dawn light was filtering through the partly closed louvres, and at some time during the night they had unconsciously moved together.

Who had first reached out for the other was not the

issue. It had happened. The only question was what to do about it.

Jed's arm was curled around her shoulder, his hand splayed against her back; one of her arms circled his taut waist while the other was tucked against his hard-muscled chest. Her fingers were touching the softly vulnerable hollow at the base of his throat, and their legs seemed to be inextricably twined together.

Her heart punched, heat crawling through her veins as the flood of desire she had no control over pooled heavily, sweetly, inside her.

He was deeply asleep, the rise and fall of his chest slow and steady, the motion lazily brushing the hardening globes of her breasts. She struggled to control the instinctive response and failed, holding her breath until she thought her lungs would burst.

She knew she should try to extricate herself, gently and carefully, so as not to wake him, end the bitter-sweet torment of this stolen intimacy, put an end to the frightening immediacy of this terrible aching need.

But her body seemed to be growing heavier, sinking deeper into the soft mattress, pressing more closely into his, electrical currents sparking from the contact of flesh against flesh, setting up convulsive shudders low down inside her. And his skin was damp, slicked with perspiration; it felt like warm sleek satin.

She ached to run both her hands over his body, re-claim all that had been hers until that terrible day just over a week ago. But she couldn't do that, she mustn't do that, mustn't give in to the intolerable temptation.

Physically, he was wrapped around her, but mentally and emotionally he had gone away, far away...

She knew the moment he woke, heard the deeper

tug of his breath, the muted, feral sound he made at the back of his throat as his hand slid down from her shoulder to spread across the curve of her buttocks, pulling her onto his immediate arousal.

Too late now to creep away without waking him. Much, much too late. Elena scarcely dared breathe, her eyes filling with sudden emotional tears.

There was no denying his urgent physical need. Or hers. But would he make love to her? And if he did would it be lust, a loveless using of her body, or would it signal a change of heart, a desire to cast out the havoc of contempt and distrust, to start again with a willingness to listen, to understand?

But shouldn't she signal her willingness to make a fresh start, let him know that for her love hadn't ended with his cruel words?

A heartbeat away from lifting her head to find his lips, whisper the words of love against them, she felt his body go rigid, heard the low-voiced self-deprecating profanity as he twisted off the bed, then padded around pulling garments from drawers before heading for the *en suite* bathroom.

She felt like dirt, and scrambled up against the pillows, wrapping her arms tightly around her body to contain the pain. The moment he'd reached full consciousness, realised what he was doing and who he was doing it with, he'd acted as if he'd found himself in bed with his arms round a bundle of evil-smelling slime!

Pushing the pain of that as far out of sight as it would go, she blinked the moisture from her eyes, controlled her breathing and swung her long legs out of bed, reaching for her wrap.

She tied the belt tightly about her small waist, the full-length mirror throwing back a wanton reflection. Rumpled blonde hair, the filmy robe doing nothing to hide her nakedness. She didn't care. There was no room for false modesty in this hateful situation. Much as she'd tried during the past long, lonely week, she hadn't been able to stop loving him. She'd been fooling herself if she'd thought for one moment that she had. But that didn't mean she'd lost all her pride.

Jed was under the shower, a cold one by the looks of things. She averted her eyes from his perfect male body, raised her voice above the sound of pounding water. 'This situation's impossible.'

'I'm not over the moon about it, either.' The gush of water stopped, and after a split second Elena steeled herself to look at him. He was wrapping a towel around his lean hips, his mouth taut, water plastering his hair to his skull, droplets gleaming on his fantastic body.

Elena clenched her hands at her sides, forbidding the instinctive, self-destructive need to touch. 'Then do something about it,' she ordered around the lump in her throat. 'Or I will.'

The towel he'd been using to rough dry his hair dropped to his side, narrowed grey eyes lacerating her. 'And what's that supposed to mean?'

She lifted her chin. He didn't frighten her. After the loss of his love, nothing could ever frighten her again. 'You could listen to me, for a start. Let me tell you exactly what happened between me and Sam.'

'No.' Angry emotion darkened his eyes. 'I don't want to hear what happened, listen to you trying to justify yourself. It sickens me.'

She couldn't reach him, she recognised hopelessly. Even if she went down on her knees and begged him to hear her out it would make no difference.

Trying to control the frustration that churned inside her, the pain of it all, she said flatly, 'If that's the way you want it. If you want to be this stubborn you can never have really loved me. And I'm not going to plead with you. But I warn you, I'm not prepared to pretend we're a loving couple when we're not. I refuse to go back to Netherhaye with you and live my life that way. So Catherine has to be told, sooner or later.'

His eyes glittered sharply. 'Later. Very much later. And you know damned well why! Or are you so wrapped up in what you want you don't care about anyone else?'

The rasped barb found its target. Her heart twisted painfully inside her. Of course she didn't want to cause Catherine any further emotional suffering, and it was an indictment of his so-called former love for her that he would so easily believe her capable of doing anything of the sort.

She closed her eyes, hiding the despised weak glitter of tears, and Jed said coldly, 'While she's here you'll act the part of a besotted wife. You managed it in bed this morning, so carrying on the act in the light of day shouldn't give you too much of a problem.'

Her eyelids batted open at that, revealing sea-blue glittery diamonds. How dared he? She hadn't consciously instigated that close embrace, and, initially at least, he'd loved every second. Wanted her—

As he wanted her now! She recognised the slight flare of his nostrils, the tightening of his jaw, the slow burn of colour across his prominent cheekbones, the drift of narrowed scorching eyes over her as-good-as-naked body. Something curled, dark and sharp, inside her. He might not love her now, but he sure as hell still desired her, she thought in bitter triumph. Something that elemental would take a long time dying.

'It's all yours.' He scooped up the clothes he'd brought in with him. 'I'll dress in the bedroom.' He brushed past, colour still darkening his face. He couldn't get away from her fast enough, she thought, untying her belt. He might hate himself for wanting her but there was nothing he could do about it.

It must have been an unconscious desire to pay him back for the pain and humiliation he'd dished out that had been behind her decision to dress the way she had. Elena walked out of the living room onto the patio, where Jed and Catherine were eating breakfast, and saw fury darken his eyes and pull his mouth into a straight, hard line, and was wickedly glad she'd clothed herself in tiny lemon-yellow silk shorts and a matching cropped halter-necked top.

'You look like a ray of morning sunshine!' Catherine beamed, clearly having forgotten and forgiven Elena's abrupt departure the evening before.

'Thank you.' She returned the older woman's smile wholeheartedly. For the duration of Catherine's stay she would play it Jed's way—with an added twist of her own! A game she would play for all she was worth, because it would be a way of showing him, and, more importantly, herself, that she was far from beaten.

She pulled a chair out from the table and sat, angling herself towards her husband, her long, shapely legs stretched out. Triumphantly she watched a muscle jerk at the side of his tough jaw as his unwilling eyes travelled the lightly tanned length of them, fastened for a millisecond on the juncture of her thighs, swept up over her naked midriff, then lingered on her breasts, lovingly cradled in sexy sheer lemon silk.

She felt her nipples peak beneath his sultry eyes, and knew he'd noticed when he abruptly pushed himself to his feet and disappeared in the direction of the kitchen, telling them tersely, 'I'll make fresh coffee.'

'My, I never thought I'd see the day when Jed got all domesticated! You're obviously very good for him!'

Not so you'd notice, Elena thought drily as Catherine laid down her cutlery and patted her round tummy. 'He insisted on making me scrambled eggs, even though everyone knows I should go on a crash diet. What are you having?'

'Just juice.' She poured some from the frosted glass jug and lay back in the sun, trying to look relaxed. Thankfully, this morning's session of feeling nauseous had only lasted a few minutes, and she'd managed to keep a glass of water down. At her mother-in-law's mock frown she added, 'I don't eat much in the morning, but, boy, do I make up for it at lunchtime!'

She buried her nose in her glass to hide the sudden onslaught of misgivings. Some time in the not too distant future Catherine would have to be told about the pregnancy. Was Jed aiming to pass Sam's child off as his own, forestalling the type of scandal he would hate? If so, he was in for an unpleasant surprise, because if there was no hope of saving their marriage she was sticking to her intention of making a clean break, the timing of which was dependent on how long it took Catherine to get back on an even keel.

Jed walked out with the fresh coffee, speaking to his mother. 'Would you like to stay here and rest up while Elena and I go down to the village for provisions?'

Elena accepted the fresh coffee he poured her and knew what he was up to. Suddenly he wasn't so sure about his own ability to act the part of a loving bridegroom in front of his parent, and in any case he probably wanted privacy to read her another riot act.

'Don't be silly, darling,' she drawled, before her mother-in-law could reply. 'Catherine hasn't come all this way to sit on her own on my patio. Why don't we go down to Cadiz, shop, have lunch, sit by the sea?' She turned her wide smile on her mother-in-law. 'You'd like that?'

'Oh, it sounds lovely, dear! Cadiz—so romantic— Francis Drake and Trafalgar—and wasn't it there that the King of Spain got his beard singed?'

'Out in the bay.' Elena smiled. 'If you extend your stay, and I hope you will, we could cross it on the ferry—the locals call it the *vapor*—and visit Puerto de Santa María. It's well worth the effort.'

Catherine beamed. Elena could see the earlier flicker of uncertainty wiped from her face. She had invited herself here, and Jed's suggestion that she spend the morning alone must have made her feel like an intruder. Jed wasn't normally insensitive where his bereaved mother was concerned. His suggestion that they leave her behind clearly showed that she was getting to him.

Elena turned a sultry smile on her stony-faced husband. 'Then that's settled, darling.' She watched his eyes go black as she lounged back in her chair, stretching her arms above her head provocatively. She hid a smile. If he accused her of flaunting herself, he'd be right. It was the only way she could think of to get her own back!

'Then perhaps you should get ready to leave?' He'd turned his back on her, staring out across the rumpled mountains. His voice was as smooth as cream, with an underlying strand of steel only she could detect.

She got lazily to her feet to obey his order. She could afford to be magnanimous; she was winning, wasn't she? Yes, the hard line of his shoulders was rigid beneath the fluid folds of the grey-green shirt he wore tucked into the waistband of his narrow-fitting stone-coloured trousers. She was really getting to him!

Swinging round to Catherine, she advised, 'Wear flatties; there'll be quite a lot of walking. And a shady hat. If you haven't brought one with you I can lend you one of mine.'

She wandered back to her room, not letting herself think beyond the trip to the capital of the province. If she was to get through the rest of Catherine's stay without going to pieces, she couldn't afford to think.

A toning button-through gauzy cotton skirt and matching short-sleeved jacket made her look decent. But she left all of the skirt buttons undone, apart from the top two, just to be provocative. She pushed her feet into thonged sandals, crammed a floppy-brimmed straw hat on her head, found another for Catherine and was ready to face Jed again.

She found him blandly urbane, excessively polite as

he drove them down the mountain, following Elena's directions as they skirted the tiny red-roofed, white-walled village that clung to the lower hillside and spilled down into the valley.

He was showing her that two could play games. His features had lost their earlier tension, and she couldn't see his eyes behind the wrap-round dark glasses he was wearing. Thankfully, Catherine's non-stop commentary on all she was seeing made any conversational efforts on her own part redundant, and her 'Oh! I could stay here for hours!' when they were in the crowded, exotic market made Elena want to hug her.

'I have a better idea.' Jed's mouth quirked humorously as he regarded the flushed, happy face of his parent. As his arms were full of bundles and carriers of fresh produce, he dipped his head to indicate a pavement café on the edge of the colourful, bustling market square. 'Wait for me there while I go back to the car and put this lot in the cool-boxes. Then we'll find somewhere nice for lunch.'

He treats her as if she were a child, Elena thought, a traumatised child who has to be handled with great care. And she was guilty of that, too, she realised, as she found herself tucking Catherine's arm through the crook of her own and murmuring cajolingly, 'We'll have coffee, shall we? It's nothing like the weak apology for the stuff you get back home!'

She registered Jed's nod of approval just before he turned away, shouldering his way through the noisy crowd of vendors and shoppers. So he approved the way she was doing as she was told, treating Catherine with kid gloves. His second order, that she act like a besotted new wife—which she had every intention of

obeying to the letter when his mother was around—
would, she vowed with a tight little smile, be something he was going to regret. She was sure he already
was!

As soon as she and Catherine were settled with their
café solo Catherine cast her eyes around the shimmering heat of the square, the shady orange trees and
the golden stone of the high, balconied buildings. 'It's
all so beautiful and vibrant, isn't it? I can understand
why you choose to live here—I hope you won't miss
it too much when you go back to Netherhaye. But I'm
sure you and Jed will spend as much time as possible
at Las Rocas.'

As things stood, she wouldn't be going back to
Netherhaye, and Jed would certainly not be spending
time with her at Las Rocas. But of course Catherine
couldn't know that; she would only be allowed to
learn the truth once she was more settled herself.

So Elena merely smiled and sipped her coffee, and
tried not to think of the way her marriage had foun-
dered, the emptiness of the loss of love, and Sam's
shadow reaching from beyond the grave, casting a
blight over what had once been so bright and beautiful.

Yet it wasn't Sam's fault, and it wasn't hers. They
had done what they'd done for what had seemed to be
sane and rational reasons at that time, and she'd truly,
truly believed that they'd failed.

No, the fault was Jed's for refusing to listen, for
thinking foul things about her, for not loving her
enough—

'Try not to be upset over your mother's decision to
make her home with me.' Catherine interrupted the
desolate drift of Elena's thoughts, thoughts she told

herself to put on the back burner for the time being, obviously mistaking her moment of solemn silence for something else.

'I could see it came as a shock to you last night. I know Susan intended writing to you about it, but she obviously hasn't got around to it.' She patted Elena's hand comfortingly. 'She was grateful and touched when you offered her a home here with you several years ago—she told me so. But, as she said, Spain seemed a long way away, and you'd flown the nest, made a huge success of your life, and she didn't want to cramp your style! She and I both agree that the younger generation don't want an old mother sitting up in a corner, probably getting in the way. Which is why I decided to move out of Netherhaye. Less responsibility for me—and lots of privacy and leeway for young lovers! And Susan and I get on famously, so I shan't be in the least bit lonely.'

How long would Catherine and her mother remain bosom friends? Elena brooded uncomfortably. When the marriage breakdown became public knowledge they would be bound to take sides—

'Why the long faces?' Jed had appeared from nowhere. He was smiling, but his tone had been tough, as if, Elena thought, he suspected her of taking this opportunity to come out with all the nasty facts of one hideously wrecked marriage.

'Girl-talk!' Catherine said brightly, standing up and tucking her handbag under her arm. 'Let's find somewhere to eat—I'm starving! And don't look so quelling.' She prodded Jed's broad chest with a forefinger. 'We girls are entitled to have our secrets!'

The wrong thing to have said, Elena thought. Jed

smiled for his mother, but his eyes, when they glanced her way, were full of contempt. He was thinking about the child she was carrying. Sam's child.

Suddenly she wanted this day to be over. Wanted Catherine safely back in England. Wanted Jed to love her again, wanted to turn the clock back...

But what she wanted she couldn't have. She followed the other two into a shady warren of narrow cobbled streets. Her spine felt like wet string and her heart felt like a lump of sludge, low down in the pit of her stomach. She didn't know how she was going to get through the rest of the day because she was hurting so much.

She had two options, she decided bleakly. One, she could drag along, looking and feeling like a wet weekend, making Catherine suspect something was very wrong, because she wasn't a teenager in a sulk but a mature woman on her honeymoon. Or, two, she could act the part of the besotted new bride, just as Jed had told her to!

Pride made her decide on the latter. Taking a deep breath, blinking away the threat of tears, she caught up with the other two, slipped between them and took Jed's arm, leaning against his shoulder, her hip and thigh brushing his as they walked.

She felt a shudder rake through his body, noted the way he tensed, and turned her grin of satisfaction into, 'There's a gorgeous restaurant overlooking the sea. We could eat outside, catch the breeze.'

Jed grunted and Catherine cried, 'Sounds good to me! Lead the way!'

Elena did, keeping up the body pressure, reminding herself that she was punishing him, repeatedly reminding herself of just why she was having to stoop to that—to take her mind off the effect the closeness of him was having on her.

When they'd seated themselves at an open-air table in a discreetly secluded corner—deliberately chosen because if she was going to make an exhibition of herself she didn't want it to be public—shaded by an awning of clambering vines, cooled by the breezes from the Atlantic, Elena could see that Jed was having a hard time controlling his temper.

The look he gave her as she slid into the seat beside his, allowing the unbuttoned edges of her skirt to fall apart to display every last inch of her long tanned legs, told her he was bitterly regretting having ordered her to pretend to be a loving wife!

Good! She gave him a brilliant smile and did her best to convince herself that she was enjoying this, getting under his skin, making him want her and despising himself for doing it, livid with her for doing it to him.

She put her hand on his arm and trailed her fingers down his skin. She felt his muscles tense and knew he wanted to brush her hand away, but he couldn't do anything of the sort under Catherine's fond maternal eye.

'Perhaps I should order, darling?' Elena murmured. 'Very few people here speak any English at all—Cadiz isn't one of those heaving internationally orientated tourist spots.'

'Whatever.' He dipped his head in seeming compliance, but she knew he didn't like her taking charge. He liked making his own decisions—witness the way he'd issued those directives on the way their future was to be conducted.

Tough! Elena consulted the menu and opted for roast vegetable salad—red peppers, tomatoes and aubergines—and clams cooked with sherry and garlic. 'Does that sound OK to you guys?'

She beckoned one of the white-coated waiters over and ordered in fluent Spanish. When she'd come out here all those years ago learning the language had been a priority, and now Catherine said admiringly, 'Is there no end to your talents?'

Smiling enigmatically, Elena plucked the shady hat from her head and ran her fingers through her hair, looking at Jed through her long, tangled lashes, her mouth pouting. 'I think you should ask my husband that!'

Recklessly flirting with him throughout the meal, Elena caught Catherine's doting, satisfied smile and guilt pushed itself right into her heart.

She was creating a fool's paradise for this nice woman. She felt ashamed of herself. The true situation, stripped of pretence and game-playing, crashed down on her then, swamping her with misery, making her feel wretched.

And she felt worse than wretched—she felt terrified—when, after Catherine had excused herself to visit the washroom, Jed took her chin in cruel fingers and told her, 'I know what you're doing and why you're doing it.'

His eyes raked her face and her heart quailed at the dark, brooding intensity of his eyes as they rested on her lips. 'Our marriage may be over in all but name, but be careful I don't grab what's so enticingly on offer. There's only so much a man can take before he forgets his scruples.'

And then his mouth was on hers, savagely parting her lips to gain admittance to the soft, sweet moisture within. She fought against the punishment—her hands balled into fists, pushing against his shoulders—fought against the flames of desire inside her, until the pressure of his lips altered, became utterly, shatteringly sensual, deeply erotic, as incredible as it had ever been when he'd loved her as much as he'd needed her, and then she opened willingly for him, fists unclenching, fingers gripping the wide span of his shoulders, blood pounding through her veins.

There was no room in her head for thought, misgivings. Her whole body had exploded with need, with wanting him, loving him. Her brain had suffered meltdown, couldn't cope with reality, wallowed in fantasy...

Until he smoothly put her away from him, advising coldly, 'Think before you play games with me. Teasing can be a two-edged sword. So watch your step, sweet wife, or you might find you've bitten off rather more than you want to chew.'

CHAPTER FIVE

ELENA put herself in the back of the car and let the conversation between mother and son up front wash right over her.

Jed had declared sexual war. That was what his kiss, his steel-edged remark had amounted to.

Men could make love without love having a look-in, he'd as good as warned her. For her it would be different, because she couldn't stop loving him, no matter how she tried, but she'd despise herself if she allowed him to use her that way.

Why had she been so stupid? Why couldn't she have acted normally, smiled and looked pleasant whenever he spoke, for Catherine's peace of mind, but kept her distance? In acting the way she had she'd pushed him to the limit of his endurance.

The way she'd behaved had been cheap and childish, and under normal circumstances she was very far from being either. But these weren't normal circumstances, she thought miserably. She'd found herself in the terrible situation of feeling hatred for the only man she'd ever really loved. Hatred, love, pain and despair were a mind-shattering combination, and had made her act in a way that made her despise herself.

She spent what was left of the afternoon showing Catherine around the property with a smile pinned on her face. Jed had said he had a raft of business telephone calls to make and had shut himself away in her study. As far as Elena was concerned he could stay there. The less she saw of him the better.

But he appeared in time for a light supper, herb omelette and fresh fruit, and afterwards Elena excused herself. 'I've got masses of watering to do, Catherine. So why don't you put your feet up and let Jed tell you about the new premises he's opening in Seville?'

And she escaped to the peace of her garden.

She'd changed into soft worn denims and a workmanlike cotton shirt, and tied her hair back with a leather thong. The everyday, pleasant chore of wandering up and down the winding paved paths, turning the hose on the stands of stately white lilies, hedges of dwarf lavender, fat pink roses and the silvery eucalyptus trees which looked wraith-like in the dusky light calmed her troubled spirits just a little.

Trying to retaliate had been an unworthy idea, serving only to inflict further hurt on both of them. Jed no longer loved her, so it was better to let it go with as much dignity as possible. The way she'd flirted and flaunted hadn't been dignified at all.

A sound at the head of the path she was working from brought her head round, her colour coming and going, her heart racing as Jed walked down the short flight of stone steps.

His face wore the closed look she had come to dread, but as he drew nearer she could see the pain in his eyes, pain he was trying to hide.

As her heart flooded with sudden compassion she despised herself anew for what she had set out to do today, and wondered if she had enough courage to tell him so. She felt as if she'd reached an important crossroads in their relationship. If she could apologise and make him believe her sincerity—

'Catherine says to say goodnight. And while I was in your study I found these.' He spoke tonelessly, cutting through her thoughts, and for the first time she noted the papers he held in his hands. 'Another came through today. Your agent is beginning to sound hysterical. Perhaps you should deal with them.'

Those neglected faxes. She shrugged, pulling in a long breath. 'I guess,' she agreed listlessly. 'Whatever it is she needs to discuss just hasn't seemed important.'

He gave her a level look. 'No? Not even something that could set the final seal of approval on your work?'

Twilight deepened the lines at either side of his mouth, shadowed his eyes, making them an enigma. She shrugged his question away. 'Look—can we talk?'

She might have imagined it, but suddenly he seemed slightly more approachable. There was so much she wanted to say to him, so much to explain. She didn't know where to begin. She could understand why he was so bitter, so angry. Putting herself in his position, she knew she would have felt the same. But it needn't be this bad for him. If only he'd allow a chink in that rock-solid armour of pride and listen to the truth!

'That's what I had in mind.' He closed the space between them. 'Shall we find somewhere to sit?' Reaching round her, he tucked the folded faxes into the back pocket of her jeans. The brush of the backs of his fingers against her buttock sent fragments of fire skittering through her veins, and all she could do was try to ignore them, rein in this helpless, hopeless yearning and follow him blindly, her sandalled feet scuffing the path, until they reached the secret rose-covered arbour, tucked away behind a bank of oleanders.

Her heart tightened in pain. She could understand his need to get well away from the house. He was probably expecting their conversation to get heated, involve raised voices. He wouldn't want Catherine to overhear. But here? Didn't he remember the evenings when they'd chosen to wander down to this lovely secluded place, sitting close together, the scent of roses perfuming the air, sharing a bottle of wine, murmuring words of love, unable to keep their hands off each other?

Or had he wiped those memories from his mind because, like her, they no longer had any meaningful place in his life?

Elena wanted to turn and head straight back for the house, to avoid hurting any more than she already was. But they had to talk, and this was the first time he'd displayed any willingness to properly discuss their situation instead of issuing untenable orders and walking away.

'I want to apologise for the way I behaved today,' she told him breathlessly, getting the words out before her courage deserted her. She sat on the far corner of the bench, knowing before he actually did it that he would sit as far away from her as he could. She knotted her hands in her lap. He wasn't making this easy. 'What I did was childish.'

'Hardly that. You came on to me like a totally adult woman. A woman who wanted sex. Like the woman who would have lapped it up early this morning, even though she knew she was carrying another man's child.'

Elena closed her eyes, locking her jaws together, taking the insult that had been delivered in a cold, hard voice. From where he stood, she deserved that. She leaned her head against the supporting pillar, her voice barely audible. 'It's not as simple as that.' How could she begin to explain the complexities of what she felt?

'No? You surprise me. But don't waste your breath apologising. The damage is done.'

She wasn't going to ask what he meant by that bald statement. She just hoped and prayed he didn't mean he was intending to give her what he believed she'd been practically begging for.

'Talking of sex,' he remarked, almost conversationally, 'and what I have reason to know is your huge appetite for it, I can't understand why you didn't invite me into your bed shortly after we met. Heaven knows, twenty-four hours after meeting you I was besotted. All I could think of was making love to you. We even discussed it,' he said drily. 'Remember? And decided the circumstances weren't right. Sam's death was still very recent. Then you had to come back here to work, because you had a deadline to meet, and I had a lot on my plate back home.

'And the days we both spent back at Netherhaye again, prior to the wedding, were hectic. So, all in all, we decided to wait until our wedding night. So romantic.' His voice levelled out with scorn. 'It would have been a damn sight more practical from your point of view if you'd dragged your willing victim into bed. That way you could have fooled me into thinking the child was mine—due to be born a little prematurely, perhaps, but nothing to get my knickers in a twist about. But perhaps you simply didn't care? After all, I was a poor second choice.'

God, but he hated her! Could love die as quickly and completely as his had, be born again in the guise of implacable, unbending hatred? She balled her hands into fists and pressed her knuckles against her temples, her head falling forwards.

If she told him what had really happened, and he actually believed she was telling the truth, would it make a scrap of difference? She didn't know, but she had to try.

She looked at him with stark appeal, took a shaky breath and told him, 'I want to tell you how Sam's baby was conceived—'

'You think I actually want to hear the sordid details?' His voice was harsh enough to raise goosebumps on every inch of her skin. He thrust himself to his feet. 'Lady, you are unreal!'

'Jed! Wait!'

But he was already striding back towards the house, finding his way through the narrow, winding paths, and much as she would have liked to stay out here, nursing wounds, she knew she had to follow.

It was almost fully dark now, the only signposts the darker undersides of the crowded plants where they encroached on the edges of the paths. Angry frustration beat through her veins, making her temples throb. It wasn't the fact that she was carrying another man's child that was responsible for this unholy mess, it was his own damned intransigence, his refusal to listen, his uncompromising hostility!

She caught up with him in the kitchen. He was pouring whisky into a tumbler. He had his back to her, and when he turned she could see he was calmer, back in control of himself and his emotions.

Well, bully for him! She wasn't. No way! Flooded with adrenalin, she stared at him, rigid with strain, sea-green eyes clashing with the cool, slightly contemptuous grey of his.

'Instead of trying to bend my ear with the details of your affair with my brother, why don't you tell me something about your first husband?'

'Liam?' Her brows pulled down in a frown. 'Why? You never wanted me to talk about him before.'

'His existence in your life wasn't important when I believed you were perfection on two legs. The past didn't matter—only our present and our future. But now we don't have a future worth the name.' He pulled a chair out from the central table and straddled it, arms leaning across the back-rest, beautifully crafted hands holding his glass loosely. He looked set for an hour or two of relaxed conversation.

Elena knew better. She brushed past him to get to the fridge to pour orange juice, to ease the tense muscles of her parched throat. She wanted to scream and shout, but knew she couldn't risk waking Catherine.

He took a mouthful of whisky. 'Well? Given the drastic alteration in my opinion of you, I'm asking now. You divorced him, you said. Why was that? Didn't he look right? Wasn't he good enough in bed? Rich enough?'

She wanted to toss her juice in his face, but her hands were shaking so badly with reined-in temper she could barely hold the glass. She slid it onto a work surface and Jed lobbed at her. 'Or was it the other way around? Did *he* divorce *you* because he, too, found out you weren't what you seemed?'

She felt her face flare with redoubled anger. Perhaps he wanted to discuss Liam because he couldn't bear to hear about her relationship with Sam. Suddenly she was too enraged to care. And what had possessed her to fall in love with someone so bitter and twisted she would never know!

He wanted a run-down on her relationship with Liam. So she'd give him one. And if it wasn't what he wanted to hear he had only himself to blame. She forced her mouth into a defiant parody of a smile. 'Liam was very good to look at.' Slightly brash, though, she could see now, from her vantage point of maturity, but she wasn't telling Jed that. 'All the girls were crazy about him and Mum thought he was God's gift—and for a woman who's as embittered as she is about the whole male sex, that's some accolade!' Her mouth gave another defiant twist. 'One of my friends threw a birthday party at some fancy club and that's where we met. He swept me off my feet, as the saying goes.'

Because she'd been desperate to be loved. Her parents had given her little of that precious commodity. Her father's job had taken him away a lot, and, in any case, he'd been too busy chasing anything in skirts to have time for his daughter. And her mother had been too busy wallowing in self-pity over the miserable state of her marriage to have time to think of her child's very real needs.

Unconsciously, she placed a hand over her tummy.

Her child wouldn't suffer because of its mother's wrecked marriage!

'And I had no complaints about his performance in bed, either,' she told him toughly. She'd been a virgin when she'd met Liam, so she'd had no experience to draw on. Only when making love with Jed had she discovered the ecstasy, the almost terrifying rapture. But she wouldn't think about that. If she did it would remind her of the love they'd found together, and lost, and she'd start crying again.

She saw his hard mouth twist, and knew she'd pierced the veneer of calm indifference. She ignored it because she couldn't afford to feel any empathy with him and stated bluntly, 'There was plenty of money, too. I kept my job on as a dogsbody in a local newspaper office, and he managed one of the city's betting shops. He drove a fast Japanese car and we spent our evenings in the best clubs. He liked me to look glamorous for him. He spent money like there was a bottomless pit of the stuff. I found out where that pit was when I came down with flu one day and left work early. I discovered his lucrative sideline in criminal activities by chance—he cloned credit cards.' She lifted her chin. 'Believe it, or not, I despise dishonesty. I despised him for the web of deceit he'd spun around me. I left him.'

'Is this true?' Jed demanded, any pretence of indifference sliding away.

'You think I'd make it up?' she asked scornfully. 'I can put grim storylines down on paper, but, whether you like it or not, I'm straightforward in my personal life.' So think on that, she tacked on silently, meeting the sudden brooding gaze with a hard, challenging stare.

'So what did you do?' he asked.

'Do?' She shook her head slowly, a slight frown pulling her brows together. It had been years since she'd thought of any of this, of Liam. She'd put it all behind her and got on with her life. She'd seen what dwelling miserably on the past had done to her mother and had wanted no part of it. 'I went to the police, of course.'

And if that made her sound hard, so be it. By then their marriage had been on the rocks. She'd been sick of the round of nightclubs, fancy restaurants, the fast crowd he belonged to, suspicious of where the stream of money was coming from, worried when he told her he'd hit a lucky gambling streak because luck didn't last.

'Mum was dead against it. She said I should simply leave him and let him get on with it. She said dirt stuck. No one would believe I hadn't been a part of it.'

'And did they?' His eyes probed her, carefully assessing her expression.

Elena lifted her shoulders wearily, reclaiming her glass of juice and swallowing it thirstily. The fire of anger had burned out and now she felt fit for nothing, mentally capitulating beneath the weight of the present situation, which was even more traumatic than the one she'd had to endure all those years ago.

She said flatly, 'After some tough questioning, yes. After the trial I came out to Spain, with little more than the clothes I stood up in—no way would I touch any of the things bought with stolen money—reverted to my maiden name and divorced him when he was two years into his prison sentence.'

It was impossible to tell what he was thinking. They'd been so in love, so close until recently, they'd been able to read each other's minds.

Not now. Not any more.

Only by the merest flicker of those darkly shadowed eyes as they touched her now wilting body did he indicate that he was aware of her presence at all.

He was probably weighing every word she'd said and deciding that her former husband had taken to crime to satisfy her ever increasing demands, that she'd coolly handed him over to the authorities before they caught up with him, foreseeing a humiliating end to the glitzy roller-coaster ride. He'd be grouping himself with Liam as the injured party. He believed that badly of her.

And he confirmed it when he said drily, 'How moral you make yourself sound. But then you're good with words. You have to be, the job you do. But there's one thing even you can't lie about, or gloss over—the fact that you married me in the full knowledge that you could be pregnant by another man.'

Anger blistered her. 'Stop this!' Her hands flew up to her head, as if to hold it on her shoulders before frustrated rage blew it away. 'Listen to yourself! I'm carrying Sam's child—nothing as vague as another man's! Sam's! Why can't you bring yourself to say his name?'

From the odd comments he'd made she was beginning to think she knew. She wasn't sure, but if she was right it would answer a whole heap of questions about his total and absolute refusal to listen to her.

'Because the thought of you and him together infuriates me,' he came back quickly, rawly.

'Infuriates?' She questioned his choice of word sharply. 'Until just now you weren't interested in my first marriage. As far as you were concerned it was unimportant. And you didn't ask if there'd been any other men in my life since my divorce. You appeared not to have a jealous bone in your body.'

Carefully, she kept her voice calm, refusing to believe there was nothing but hatred behind that stony façade, hoping, almost against hope, that she could find a way to get through to him. 'Just as I didn't want, or need, to know who you might have shared a bed with before we met. I believed our future was all that mattered, not what might or might not have happened in the past. I'm sure you felt that way, too.'

He shrugged, impatience highlighting his eyes now. 'I see no point in rehashing this.'

'Probably not,' she conceded, 'but there is one. Ask yourself if you'd have felt so badly—so betrayed,' she granted him, 'if this baby had been an accident, fathered by any other man. Some man, say, I'd had a brief and meaningless affair with before I met you. And then ask yourself why you categorically refuse to let me tell you what really happened between me and Sam.'

'I would have thought that was glaringly obvious.' He spoke drily but there was a frown-line between his eyes now. Was he thinking about what she'd said? Really thinking instead of letting his emotions get in the way of logic?

'This tortured conversation is getting us nowhere.' He put his empty glass down on the drainer, and she knew that if she let him go she would have lost this last opportunity to get through to him. He would never again stand still long enough to have a meaningful discussion about anything.

As he walked to the door she said firmly, 'Sam wasn't my lover. He was my friend, nothing more. I wanted a child; Sam donated the sperm. A completely clinical happening. Check with the clinic in London if you don't believe me!'

He went very still, as if her words had frozen him. And then he turned, slowly. Something like ridicule looked out of his eyes. 'I applaud your inventive imagination. It gets you into the bestseller lists but it won't get you anywhere with me.'

Although the hope of finally getting through to him had been slender almost to the point of invisibility, it hurt like hell now she'd lost it. She pushed past him, out of the room, before he could see the desolation on her face, went to her room and closed the door.

Sleepless hours later she heard him go into the second guest room, and something hard and dark clawed at her heart. Not even for the look of things where Catherine was concerned could he bring himself to share the air she breathed, let alone this bed.

Finally she'd been able to tell him the truth about her baby's conception. But he didn't believe her.

She turned her face to the pillow. It didn't matter. Nothing mattered, did it?

CHAPTER SIX

'CONGRATULATIONS, Elena! What a clever little duck you are!' Catherine cried as Elena ventured out onto the terrace at ten-thirty the next morning. 'Jed's been telling me all about it.'

Elena pushed her hands into the deep pockets of her common or garden cotton skirt and tried to look as if she knew what her mother-in-law was talking about. She'd overslept, woken feeling queasy as usual, and dressed down, dowdily even.

She glanced across the terrace to where Jed was sprawled out on a lounger, yesterday's newspaper over his face to protect it from the fierce rays of the sun, wearing frayed denim shorts and nothing else.

Elena swallowed a constriction in her throat. He had a beautiful body, tanned all over, a smooth, slick skin, not too hairy, and not bulging with muscles, either, but honed and hard, superbly fit.

Almost as if he'd sensed her eyes on him, Jed explained lazily, 'I was telling her about the frantic faxes from your agent about the awards ceremony and your latest book being short-listed.' He plucked the paper from his face and swung his bare feet to the floor, pushing a hand through his hair, making it stick up in soft spikes which invited the touch of her fingers.

Firmly, she pulled her dark glasses from a capacious skirt pocket and put them on. She didn't dare let him look at her eyes because he'd surely see the starkness of unwilling need there. She wouldn't let him know that every time she looked at the man who thought she was a deceitful little liar, totally devoid of morals, her body stirred with that desperate, consuming need. She still had her pride, if little else in the way of self-defence. She'd do her damnedest to hang onto it.

'And as we'll have to return to London to attend, I've booked us on the same flight back as Ma. Luckily there were spare seats.'

Catherine was saying something about enjoying the flight home so much more if she wasn't going to be on her own. Elena wasn't listening properly. She wasn't in the mood to concentrate on the older woman's happy chatter.

He was doing it again, mapping her life out for her, telling her what to do and when to do it, regardless of her feelings, not even asking her what she wanted. No doubt he'd decided she didn't merit that courtesy.

And possibly the worst thing—the almost unbearably frustrating thing—was her complete inability to do anything about it. Not in front of Catherine, anyway.

She swung away, her shoulders tight with tension, walking to the edge of the terrace, feeling the hot Andalucian breeze mould her cotton top to her body, lifting her head to inhale the spiritually healing scent of her garden flowers, the more astringent perfume of mountain herbs.

Life had been so uncomplicated once. She'd had it all—her home in a country she'd come to love for its vibrancy and passion, this spectacular view, a highly successful career. The only thing to mar it had been the growing and savagely compelling need to hold her own child in her arms.

It was ironic that the child that was now growing inside her was the reason for her present ejection from the paradise she'd found in Jed's love.

'Why don't you finalise the details with your agent, darling?' He'd come to stand beside her. He put a hand on her shoulder. His touch branded her. She wanted to swipe his hand away, tell him not to call her darling because he didn't mean it, tell him to stop torturing her!

She turned her head sharply, her breath catching explosively in her throat, her hair flying around her shoulders. His slight warning frown told her *Not in front of Catherine*, but he sounded totally laid back when he added, 'We've only a couple more days here, so Ma and I will get out from under your feet. We'll go and explore the village, potter around, give you time to pack and make arrangements for closing the house up.'

He was giving her a breathing space. That, at least, was something to be grateful for. Somehow she managed to make all the right noises, to smile, even, telling them about another village, further down the valley, where there were the ruins of a castle and a thirteenth-century church, expressing rather vague and insincere regrets that she was unable to accompany them, escaping at last to the privacy of her study, feeling the blessed silence of her home settle around her.

She sat at her desk and sank her head into her hands. She had a few precious hours alone, no need to play-act for Catherine's benefit. Thoughtfully, Jed had given her that time. But probably not for her benefit, she decided with a shuddery sigh. He must have realised the strain she was under and hadn't wanted her to explode in front of his mother and ruin the poor woman's illusions.

And he could escape, too, just for a few hours. Get away from the woman he'd once loved and now regarded with contempt and distrust.

She lifted her head, pushed her hair away from her face with one hand, reached for the phone with the other and began to dial her agent's London number.

Netherhaye was as lovely as Elena remembered it. A sprawling edifice of golden stone, drowsing in the late afternoon sun, the lovely house managed to insert a sharp finger of sadness into her heart. Had her marriage still been strong, beautiful and true, she would have looked forward to their sharing their time between here and Las Rocas.

But she mustn't think like that, she told herself. And made herself concentrate on the housekeeper's effusive greetings. Edith Simms was a fixture, Catherine had told her. Efficient, willing, very likeable—almost part of the family.

She pushed the unwelcome feeling of sadness out of the way. She'd coped well these last few days, but only because she'd known she had to, and the hundred and one things she'd had to do—and a few dozen more that had been pure invention—before she could leave Las Rocas had helped more than anyone would ever know.

But she wouldn't be away from Spain for too long, she assured herself. The only way into the future was to smother all her emotions and go forward, get on with her life. But that would have to wait until after the ceremony.

'I've made the master suite ready for you and Mrs Nolan,' Edith said to Jed, smiling comfortably, convinced she'd done the right thing. Elena wondered what she'd think if she knew the truth, that Jed couldn't bear the sight of his new bride, that the thought of sharing a bedroom with her made him shudder.

'Thank you, Edith.' Jed's features were impassive. 'I'll take the cases up—no need to get your husband in from the gardens. Is he still managing?'

'Oh, yes, very well. It's the winter when his arthritis plays up and makes things difficult. Come the warm weather and he's right as ninepence.'

'Good.' Jed smiled down into the housekeeper's homely face. 'I'll have a word with him about getting a lad in to do the heavier work—and don't worry about him starting to feel old and redundant. I'll make sure he knows he's the gaffer and that we need his valuable experience and know-how.'

'Thank you, Mr Nolan, sir!' Edith breathed, her faded brown eyes like an adoring spaniel's as Jed strode away to fetch the cases from the car. Elena told herself not to go soft and start admiring his understanding and compassion. He'd shown not a scrap where she was concerned.

'And Susan Keele asked you to phone just as soon as you had a moment.' The housekeeper had turned to Catherine, and Catherine's eyes went round and wide, like an excited child's.

'She must have some definite news about the cottage! How wonderful! I'll phone right away. You'll want to speak to her, too, Elena. Let's go through to the little sitting room.'

Of all the many rooms at Netherhaye this was one of Elena's favourites. Comfy armchairs, slightly the worse for wear, were grouped around a stone hearth where apple logs burned brightly in the colder weather. Chunky little oak tables were piled with gardening books and magazines, and Marjory Allingham prints hung on the faded ochre walls, and there was a view of the mysteriously inviting edges of Catherine's water garden from the mullioned window.

'Here—' Catherine held out the receiver. 'It's ringing out. You speak to her first.'

Elena took it and began to explain why she and Jed had returned from Spain much sooner than expected.

'Well, it's nice to be on the short-list, I suppose, but a pity to spoil your honeymoon,' Susan dismissed, not to Elena's very great surprise. Her mother had never been much interested in what her daughter did—apart from her marriages. Susan wanted her settled so she could cross her off her list of things to worry about. Elena shuddered to think what her mother's reaction would be when she learned the truth.

'The sale's going through that end, and I've put this house on the market.' Now she was all enthusiasm, practically buzzing with it. 'I should have made a move years and years ago—got away from bad memories—but I never could seem to be able to face it. I'm really looking forward to sharing that cottage with Catherine. I do admire her. The way she coped with Sam's death made me see that life goes on.'

After five more minutes in the same vein, Elena handed over to Catherine and went to see what Jed had done about their sleeping arrangements, wondering if her mother could be right and Catherine was far stronger than they'd thought.

It was worth thinking about. Maybe they didn't need to pussyfoot around her quite so much. Maybe she could take the news of the breakdown of their marriage without going to pieces.

Maybe she could tell her the truth without feeling too guilty...

She found Jed in the beautifully furnished, elegantly decorated master suite. He was staring out of one of the tall windows and didn't turn, much less greet her when she closed the panelled door behind her. Well, what else had she expected?

She said tonelessly, detachedly pleased she was at last winning the battle with her emotions, pushing them down, grinding them out of sight with a metaphorical heel, 'I can use the room I had when I stayed here before.' And refused to let herself remember how extraordinarily wonderful that time of falling so deeply in love had been.

'No.' Still he didn't turn to face her, seeming to find the view of the gardens and the rolling countryside beyond irresistible. 'Not until Catherine's settled into the cottage. And by then I'll be making myself scarce. I told you I would, remember? Then you can have the whole damned place to yourself!'

She heard the note of angry exasperation but didn't let herself take any pleasure from the fact that she could still provoke some emotion. She told herself she was now completely indifferent. It was over. Over and finished. And because it was it had to be tidied away, put neatly out of sight, and then it could be forgotten.

'I'm sorry, but I won't go along with that,' she told

him in a clear, cool voice. 'You decided we'd play at being the ideal happy couple. I wasn't consulted. So you can play-act on your own, because after that wretched awards ceremony I'm out of here.'

'No.' He did turn then. Abruptly, almost clumsily. She saw the harsh lines of strain on his tough features and refused to betray her hard-won indifference by feeling any compassion for him at all. He had brought it on himself by refusing to believe that there had been nothing more than a clinical arrangement between her and his brother. 'Have you no consideration for Catherine's feelings? And what about the child? Doesn't he or she deserve the care of two parents? I know Sam would have wanted that.'

Pallor spread beneath his tan, and intuitively she knew what it had cost him to mention his brother in this context. She said, more gently than she'd intended, 'I'm sorry, but I can't agree with you on that, either. Sam wouldn't have wanted his child brought up by parents who loathed each other.' She spread her hands in a gesture that said how hopeless the situation was. 'You say we could be polite and pleasant to each other in the company of others. But think about it. Life would become intolerable and the cracks would start to show—Sam wouldn't have wanted us to suffer that way.'

She probed the hard grey eyes, wondering if she was getting through to him. Impossible to tell. He seemed to have blanked off, the earlier flare of emotion under tight control. 'I'm perfectly capable of caring for my child on my own. I don't need support, financial or otherwise. And remember, I'm not a silly little girl; I've been making my own decisions for many years now. And as for Catherine, I think she deserves to be told. Not brutally, of course, but gently. I'm beginning to believe she's stronger than you think.'

He turned back to his contemplation of the view, hands thrust into the pockets of his trousers. 'You're getting good at doing this, aren't you?'

'Doing what?' She didn't understand.

'Saying goodbye and moving on.' Hard shoulders lifted in a shrug. 'Liam, Sam, me.'

'This is different,' she said quickly, without thinking, her feelings for this man fighting to surface.

'Is it?' It was his turn to display utter, drawling indifference. 'Now why is that?'

'Because I love you.'

She tried to bite back the words but they'd already escaped her. Why the purple petunias had she used the present tense?

Because her emotions were stronger than her will to control them.

She left the room as quickly and quietly as she could, knowing that the stand she'd so decisively made had been fatally undermined by those four un-thinking words.

She was going to have to try harder. Much, much harder.

The oak-panelled breakfast room was filled with morn-ing sunlight when Elena walked in, feeling groggy. Not so much morning sickness but the aftermath of a hatefully restless night.

Jed had refused to hear of her moving out of the master suite. He'd pointed her at the huge double bed, tossed one of the pillows and a light blanket onto the Edwardian chaise longue beneath one of the windows and spent the night there, sleeping like a baby as far as she could tell, while she'd lain in the big lonely bed, stiff as a board, not letting herself toss and turn because he might wake and guess the reason for her restlessness.

And now he was at the breakfast table, finishing off with toast and marmalade, unfairly hunky in a soft white T-shirt and narrow, scuffed black denims.

He laid aside his newspaper and remarked blandly, 'I told Edith you wouldn't want a cooked breakfast. Help yourself to juice and toast—if you're ready for it. Should I ring for fresh coffee?'

She shook her head, sitting opposite him, smoothing out the full skirts of the tan-coloured cotton dress she was wearing, pleating the fabric between her fingers as he filled a glass with orange juice and pushed it towards her with the tip of his finger.

If he was going to act like a polite stranger, pretend nothing had happened to turn lovers into enemies, then she'd go along with it. For now. Frankly, she didn't feel up to fighting, restating her decision to leave him and make a clean break. It would have to wait until she felt better able to handle it. Once the awards ceremony was out of the way she could concentrate on organising the rest of her life.

He'd picked up his paper again, but after a few minutes of intolerable silence, when the only sound appeared to be the bumping of her heart against her ribcage, he lowered it and told her, 'Catherine's taken herself down to the cottage. Apparently the Fletchers moved out a couple of days ago. Contracts won't be exchanged for another six weeks or so, but she couldn't wait to look round the garden and make plans for transforming it.'

Six weeks of pretending to be the ecstatic new bride, then Lord knew how much longer staying meekly here, playing the role of the understanding wife, while he made himself scarce, immersed himself in business.

That was his decision. It wasn't, and never could be, hers. Her stomach lurched, an uneasy prelude to ejecting the few sips of juice she'd swallowed. She pushed the glass away.

'I'll be in the garden if you want me.' He folded the paper and put it to one side, his tone telling her he knew she wouldn't. 'I'll be helping Simms trim the yew hedges and breaking the news that he's to have permanent help.' He stood up, looked at his watch. 'I suggest you register with the local GP. Edith will let you have the surgery's number. Make an appointment to have a check-up. It's past time you did.'

And he left the room.

She hadn't said a word, Elena realised as deep silence settled around her. Not a single one. Was this how Jed saw their future? He dictating, she accepting, turning into a mouse?

Pushing herself to her feet, she knew she couldn't let that happen. She went to find Edith.

Two hours later she followed the sound of the electric hedge-cutter and found Jed on a step-ladder, neatening off the top of the ten-foot high ancient yew hedges that surrounded Catherine's formal rose garden.

Simms said, 'Nice to see you again, Mrs Nolan—

grand day isn't it?' He smiled at her and wheeled a barrow of trimmings away, and Jed came down the steps, switching off the noisy implement, a slight frown lowering his straight black brows.

He looked gorgeous. All man and touchable. Very, very touchable. Heat, hard work, sweat and hedge-dust had left smudges on his face, rumpled up his hair and created damp and grubby patches on his old T-shirt.

Elena swallowed convulsively but kept her head high, her face serene. And of course he was looking puzzled, wondering why she was so glossy, so packaged.

She'd arranged her pale hair at the nape of her neck, in a smooth, cool style, fixed tiny gold studs into the lobes of her ears and was wearing a suit he hadn't seen before—straw-coloured linen, with a short-sleeved, nipped-waist, collarless jacket over a straight skirt that ended two inches above her knees—and plain, slightly darker-toned high heels.

She said, as if reciting from a list, 'I've registered with Greenway and I've arranged for a check-up in four days' time.' The morning of the awards ceremony. And before he could give her a verbal pat on the head for being a good girl and doing as she'd been told, she said, in the same breath, 'Edith said it was all right for me to borrow the Astra. So I'll head for London now. I managed to get a room at my usual hotel—a lucky late cancellation—and I'll see you back here in three days' time.'

She heard him pull in his breath as she turned to go, and a second later his voice made her pause. 'Running away, Elena?'

She swung back. Never let it be said she hadn't the

courage to look him in the eye. 'No. Shopping. I'd like something extra special to wear for the ceremony. You never know, I might win. And if I don't, I'll want to go down with all flags flying. Besides—' she did what he'd done to her at breakfast: looked pointedly at her watch, and wondered if he felt as she had done—surplus to requirements '—I need to see my editor and my agent. I'm sure you can square my flit with Catherine. She at least understands that I have a life.' She lobbed him a flinty smile. 'You should be grateful. I'm sparing you my noxious company for three whole days. And nights.'

She turned again and walked down the path. Her spine was as straight as it could possibly go, but, boy, was it tingling! She half expected him to bounce up behind her and grab her, lock her in the attic, if that was what it took, and keep her there until a situation arose that demanded she be brought out and paraded— a new bride doll with a painted smile and a puppet master to pull her strings.

But he did no such thing. Of course he didn't. He let her go.

The hotel she always used when she flew into London to see her publisher was comfortable and unpretentious. It suited her. Or had done.

Tonight she couldn't settle. Jed haunted her mind and filled her heart. Memories of the good times, those special, wonderful, loving times, kept coming back, resurfacing seconds after she'd thought she'd pushed them back into oblivion. The bad times, too, were ever present, tormenting her.

Since arriving she'd made an appointment to meet

with her editor tomorrow, and another to have lunch with her agent the day after that. The rest of the time would be spent shopping for that perfect dress, shoes to wear with it, maybe a new perfume.

She'd get her hair trimmed. And what about a facial? Manicure? Browse through the bookshops. Why not? Anything to fill the hours, occupy her mind.

But the nights—what was she to do about the nights? She frowned at the television set, talking to itself in a corner of the room, picked up the remote control and zapped it off. She took herself to bed and tried to read, but the words didn't make any sense at all.

She had shown Jed that she had a mind of her own, that she wasn't prepared to dance to his mournful tune, live a lie into the foreseeable future. She'd made her stand and escaped an intolerable situation.

This trip to London hadn't been about buying new clothes, it had been about escape. But she could never escape, no matter how far she ran, not while he was still firmly in her heart.

CHAPTER SEVEN

ELENA fixed the diamond ear-studs with steady fingers. Set in ornate, chunky gold, they matched the bracelet around her slender wrist. Jed's wedding gift to her. She'd leave these lovely things behind at Netherhaye when all this was over. She had only decided to wear them tonight because they were the perfect complement to her dress.

She stood back, looking at her reflection in the full-length mirror. She'd do. No ballooning bulge in the tummy region yet, although during her check-up Greenway had assured her it wouldn't be long before it appeared!

But for now the champagne-coloured satin sheath lovingly caressed every softly rounded curve. Ending a few inches above her knees, it made her look very leggy, and the deeply scooped top, suspended only by the thinnest of shoestring straps, made her breasts look fuller than they were. Or maybe that was down to her condition?

She'd left her hair loose tonight, a shimmering golden sweep curving down to her shoulders, and for once her make-up couldn't be faulted. She looked, she decided dispassionately, like a sophisticated, sexy, mature professional woman. It was the look she had deliberately set out to achieve.

And, thankfully, not a butterfly in sight.

Jed was to accompany her to the awards ceremony.

Even she had had to admit that it would look odd if he didn't. There'd been a few qualms, though, when he'd told her that he'd booked a suite for the night in the up-market hotel where the ceremony was to be held, but he'd told her glacially, 'I don't suppose you'd want to travel up to town in your glad rags, or face the drive back in the small hours. The suite has two bedrooms and a sitting room, so we should be able to share it without coming to blows.'

So she'd handle being here with him without the buffer of Catherine's company and Edith's to-ings and fro-ings. She felt calm enough right now to be sure of that.

His perfunctory tap on the door of her bedroom told her it was time to go. She pushed her feet into pale bronze-coloured high heels and straightened her shoulders. She wasn't looking forward to this evening, but she'd grit her teeth and get through it in style.

He was ready and waiting in the ultra-modern, elegantly furnished but impersonal sitting room, and as his eyes swept over her body then back to her face she saw his hard jaw tighten.

'You look very beautiful, Elena.'

'Thank you.' She took the clipped compliment as calmly as she could. He was simply being polite. And she could have said the same of him, but she'd bite her tongue out before she'd repay the compliment.

He looked better than good whatever he wore, but in his black dinner suit he looked spectacular. Sizzlingly handsome yet challengingly remote. He could shatter her senses but she wouldn't let him.

Deftly, she swept up her evening purse from the side table where she'd left it earlier. She caught the glimmer of gold from her wide wedding band and misery welled up inside her.

For a moment it swamped her, but she resolutely stamped it down. And then Jed said, in a rough, tough voice she barely recognised, 'Believe it or not, whichever way it goes tonight, I'm proud of your achievements.'

Dipping her head in brief acknowledgement, she blinked furiously. It would be easier on her if he kept his mouth shut. She didn't want his compliments or his praise. In this hateful situation they hurt far too much.

And she would not cry! Wouldn't let herself be that weak! He certainly knew how to get to her, twist the knife and bring her pain. Though, to give him his due, he probably hadn't meant to.

He didn't realise how much he could hurt her, how desperately she wanted things to be as they had been, or how desperately she was trying not to want it.

She bit her lip as she preceded him into the lift. And Jed chided gently, 'Do that much longer and you won't have any lipstick left.' He took her hand as the lift settled to a well-bred halt and the doors slid open. 'There's no need to be nervous. I'm rooting for you— whatever the panel of judges have decided. I admit I don't read the genre, but I *have* read your work, and for my money I fail to see how anyone else can come near you!'

If things had been different she'd have squeezed his hand, smiled up into his eyes and told him he was biased. And kissed him for his kindness.

As it was her fingers lay coldly within his, any reply she might have made stuck in her throat. He had only taken her hand because they were now on public show and the pretence had to go on.

She wasn't nervous about tonight, but he thought she was and so had put his negative feelings for her behind him, trying to make her feel better, calm her down. But he was only making it worse, reminding her that at heart he was a good man, caring and compassionate.

She had lost all that, and the loss was once again sharpening its claws on her heart. She was finding it impossible to bear.

But tonight—whichever way the award went—she was on show. She couldn't turn tail and head back to her room, no matter how desperately she wanted to do just that. She couldn't let him down. The effort of getting through the evening was probably the last thing she would ever be able to do for him.

'You look a star!' Trish, her agent, cried excitedly.

Paula, her more down-to-earth editor, stated, 'Don't worry about the competition, El. None of them hold a candle, I promise.'

'That's exactly what I've been telling her!' Jed slipped an arm around her waist and tugged her against his side.

Elena wanted to scream. Didn't he know what he was doing to her? No, of course he didn't. He thought he was giving her reassurance, and the way he was holding her was nothing but playing to the gallery.

Straightening out her brain, she made the introductions, noticed the way the two women—and every other woman in the room—ate him up with their eyes, and wondered again how he could ever believe he could come second-best to any man.

A lavish, pre-ceremony dinner was to be served in this glittering room, and the four of them were sharing a table. The food, so everyone said, was superb, and there seemed to be an endless supply of champagne. And Jed was being ultra-supportive, acting the part of the adoring husband, making her insides quiver with longing for the impossible, making it impossible for her to eat a thing.

'I think, under the circumstances, one small glass of champagne would be permissible,' he said softly, while their dinner companions had their heads together discussing publishing trends. He poured for her, and put the cool stem of the glass between her fingers.

She didn't want it. She'd stuck to spring water all evening, and wasn't in a champagne mood in any case. He probably thought she needed the Dutch courage, because all attention was beginning to turn to the small raised dais where the guest speaker was taking up his place to present the awards.

Elena didn't listen to a word. At any other time during her writing career she would have been ecstatic to have had a work of hers short-listed for the prestigious Golden Gargoyle Award, given for the best horror novel published in the preceding year.

Now it seemed monumentally unimportant. She had only agreed to attend tonight because to have stayed away would have been a snub. In the future she would need her career. She was determined that her fatherless child would have every possible advantage.

Tumultuous applause forced her into an awareness that the evening was coming to its end, at least as far as the awards were concerned. And then Jed put his hands on either side of her waist and helped her to her feet. Smiling into her bemused eyes, he murmured, 'Congratulations! Go get it, sweetheart. I hope you rehearsed your speech!'

Only then did it sink in that *At the Rising of the Moon* had won her the coveted award. Walking towards the dais, she wondered why she couldn't feel even the tiniest flicker of elation, the smallest smidgen of professional pride. And then she told herself she knew damn well why she didn't, and hoped to goodness the bleak knowledge didn't show in her face. Professional achievement was nothing compared to Jed's love.

She had one, but she had lost the other.

Somehow she managed to smile and say a few words. Weaving her way back through the body of the room, she was waylaid by people who wanted to congratulate her so often she was beginning to think she'd never make it back to their table before breakfast!

When she finally made it Jed was waiting, watching her with pride. She had to admit it looked genuine, but then he'd been putting on a remarkably polished performance all evening.

Trisha and Paula gave her enormous hugs, and Paula said, 'Trish and I are now going to circulate— give you two some time on your own. You are still on your honeymoon, after all!'

They melted away, glasses firmly in hand, and Jed said tonelessly, 'Shall we do the rounds? I'm sure there are still people who'd like to congratulate you.'

Mutely, Elena shook her head. She wanted out. Wanted the whole charade over and done with. Tears suddenly misted her eyes. She stared down at the glittering trophy clasped in her hands so that he wouldn't see how emotional she had suddenly and infuriatingly become.

There had been times, just recently, when she'd believed she had come to terms with losing this man. This wasn't one of them. The evening had taken its toll, and heaven only knew what would happen if they stayed on, proud, adoring husband, ecstatically happy wife, on display for public consumption. She'd probably go to pieces and make an utter fool of herself. She'd had as much of this cruel fantasy as she could take.

'I'd rather go to bed,' she confessed wearily, not meeting his eyes. 'Pull the sheets over my head and wake up feeling halfway normal.'

'Fine.' He put a hand under her elbow and led her from the room. He'd sounded drained, too.

They rode the lift in silence, the tension almost strident as they entered the suite. The distance across the pale sage-green carpeting to her bedroom suddenly seemed immense. Elena didn't know if her shaky legs would carry her that far. Lack of food, she supposed, and thrust her fingers through her hair.

The trophy fell to the floor and bounced on the carpet, and Jed turned, frowning darkly. 'Are you all right?'

The last thing she wanted was him fussing over her, pretending to care. There'd been enough pretence this evening to last her several lifetimes.

She looked at him through tangled dark lashes, her lids too heavy to open wide, and tried to tell him she was fine. But she couldn't get the words out. She swallowed hard, then moistened her glossy lips to see if that would help, and watched him watch the convulsive movement of her throat, then lift narrowed eyes to her mouth and fasten them on her own.

She saw the slow burn begin deep in the smoky irises and drew in her breath sharply, totally and stingingly aware of him, of this silent seclusion. He wanted her. It was there in his eyes, in the tightness of the line of his mouth. He wanted her and she needed him...

'Get to bed,' he said roughly. 'You look done in.' He turned, retrieved the trophy and put it down on a coffee table. Elena swayed on her feet.

The split second of danger was over. He'd successfully fought it off. But she could still feel the dark sting of it pulsing through her veins. All the wanting, all the need, had practically solidified into something she could reach out and touch. Emotion powered through her as she faced the acres of carpet, the bedroom door that seemed to shimmer and shift, recede even further into the distance.

She swayed dizzily, and strong hands grasped her shoulders, steadying her, holding her. 'You're ill?' he demanded, using one hand to lift her chin and read the truth in her eyes.

'No,' she whispered threadily, deploring the weak rush of tears to her eyes, the way her lips parted helplessly as he gently brushed the moisture away with the ball of his thumb.

'Don't! I can't bear to see you cry,' he said rawly. 'Tonight you looked so beautiful, so assured. I want you to stay that way. Believe it or not, I don't want you to be unhappy.' He folded his arms around her, holding her just a little away from him, as if he wanted to make sure that their bodies didn't actually touch. 'I thought I did, but now I know I can't hate you that much.'

A primitive spurt of anger made her pull in a ragged breath. She felt humiliated. His emotions where she was concerned weren't powerful enough to even let him hate her properly! Had his former so-called love for her been similarly lukewarm? Was that the reason he'd been able to shut her out of his heart so damned easily? Had refusing to believe the truth about her baby's conception been the easy way out for him?

She felt weak and shaken, but she balled her hands into fists and pushed feebly at his chest. He ignored her childishly ineffectual blows and scooped her up off her feet. 'You're physically and emotionally exhausted,' he told her in a matter-of-fact near monotone as he carried her towards the door to her bedroom. 'I'll see you into bed and ask Room Service for warm milk and toast. That should help you sleep. You were far too hyped up to eat anything at dinner.'

She didn't want his spurious kindness, his warm milk, or his dratted attention to what he would see as his precious duty! She wanted... She needed...

A fierce rush of adrenalin pushed all caution to the winds. She squirmed hectically against him, struggling to get back on her own two feet, shrieking, 'Let go of me! Stop being such an odious holier than thou, pompous, prattish little gentleman!'

She squirmed more furiously, wriggling and pushing against him, her narrow skirt riding high on her thighs, her face scarlet with temper, outrage and frustration, her breath coming in short, sharp gasps, unaware until it was too late—far too late—of the fine tremors that shook his lean, hard frame, of the dangerous glitter of fiery intent in eyes that were suddenly narrowed, black with savage emotion.

'I can be as ungentlemanly as you like, sweetheart, believe me!'

His hands tightened on her body as he shouldered open the bedroom door and strode to the bed. He tumbled her onto the covers, one hand fastening her wrists together above her head, his darkly glittering eyes making a quick inventory of her body, sweeping up the length of her silk panty-hose-clad legs to the scrumple of champagne satin around her hips and on to the rapid rise and fall of her breasts, their swollen peaks thrusting against the slithery satin that barely contained them now.

And back down again, more slowly. Much more slowly. Caressing her. Elena shuddered helplessly as desire made a pool of liquid heat inside her. She stopped breathing as she followed the journey his eyes were making, her flesh quivering in mindless anticipation because each slow stroke of his eyes was like the physical touch of his lean, sensual fingers.

She could feel the tension in him, almost feel the tremors that shook his taut frame, smell the raw, hot male scent of him. Slowly he released her wrists, and her body conquered what was left of her mind and moved luxuriously, sensuously, beneath the burning drift of his eyes, drugged eyes, that swept slowly up to lock with hers.

'Yes,' he said softly. 'Now.' He removed his jacket and tossed it carelessly aside, ripping away his shirt to reveal muscles clenched with need, a need that raged tempestuously through her, too. A need she understood, found impossible to deny, a need she answered as she lifted her arms to him in silent invitation.

With boneless grace he joined her, taking her hands and winding them around his neck, groaning deeply as her fingers stroked his nape. Lovingly, they feathered down his throat, down to the hectic pulse-beat at the base.

She loved him, always would. Her body craved him with a hunger that was out of control. With a tiny mew of rapture she wriggled closer, pressing her breasts against his naked chest, feeling the race of his heartbeats as he slid one tiny strap away from her shoulder and then the other.

Yes! She needed skin to skin, flesh to burning flesh. And, as ever, he knew what she wanted because that was what he wanted, too.

He closed the tiny gap between their mouths and she opened for him, inviting the raging hunger of his kiss, shuddering all over. Her fingers were digging into his back as he slid a hand up the length of her thigh and tugged impatiently at the waist of her panty-hose, sliding the silk away from her body, his breath catching as his touch revealed she was wearing nothing else beneath her dress.

She hadn't dressed for seduction. The lines of a bra and panties showing beneath the clinging satin would have spoiled the svelte impression. Yet seduction was happening here, she thought muzzily. But who was seducing whom?

It didn't matter. Nothing mattered now but this, this togetherness. He reached behind her to find the concealed zipper of her dress, turned her over and stripped the fabric from her heated body.

She endured the slow stroke of his hands as they moulded her from her shoulders down to her thighs for as long as she could bear the deliriously rising excitement inside her, then turned with a sign of frustrated need, arching her body into his.

He kissed her slowly, her mouth, her eyelids, the hollow of her neck, taking his time, making her take hers, just as he had done so many times before, not rushing things in spite of the urgency of his body's response.

A wild coupling to assuage an urgent need had never been his way with her. He was finding the most circuitous route to heaven, making sure the arrival would be as sublime for her as it was for him, just as he had done in the days when he had loved her.

'Sweetheart,' he murmured throatily as he lifted his head from her breasts, his eyes hazed with desire. 'This is so unbelievable. What you do to me...'

Even the words were the same, almost incoherent endearments, words that told her of the depth of his love. Only this wasn't love.

A tiny icy shiver froze her veins. It congealed her blood, shocked her into recognition of what was actually happening here.

She still loved him, couldn't stop no matter how she tried. Physically and emotionally she would always be his. But he hated her—not enough to wish her harm, he'd said—but implacably, eternally.

This, this happening, was simply sex. Perhaps, right now, he believed they could use each other and survive the encounter unscathed.

But she knew differently. Tonight, for all sorts of reasons, she'd pushed him beyond endurance. Lots of men lost sight of their scruples as soon as they dropped their trousers. But not Jed. He would despise himself. And she would despise *herself* for letting it happen, actively encouraging him.

They would despise each other and fatally spoil the memories that were left of how they had loved each other once.

As his fingers found the sweet moistness that told him she was more than ready for him she knew she had to stop this, for both their sakes.

Wriggling away from him was the hardest thing she'd ever do, but she had to do it. Pushing herself back against the heaped pillows, reaching for her discarded dress, she held the satin against her breasts and lied recklessly, 'If you want sex, just go ahead. I won't stop you. But I'm warning you, there'll be a difference. You see, I don't love you any more. How can I love a man who thinks I'm a liar? It will be just like scratching an itch.'

Being cruel to be kind just wasn't in it, she conceded bleakly as she watched his features display at first blank incredulity, followed by black anger, then cold contempt.

And then he swung himself to his feet, and she watched him walk away and ached to call him back, retract those hateful, hateful words, and pushed her knuckles against her teeth to stop the anguished cry escaping.

CHAPTER EIGHT

GETTING out of bed the following morning took a monumental effort of will. After what had happened last night Elena didn't know how she was going to face Jed; she only knew she had to.

They couldn't go on like this. Somehow she had to make him understand that she couldn't and wouldn't play her part in the painful charade he had so arbitrarily decided on, and this morning, before they set out for Netherhaye, was the perfect opportunity.

She dressed in the cotton trousers and top she'd travelled down in, stuffed the award trophy and the satin designer gown any old how into her overnight bag, and forced herself to walk through into the sitting room.

Jed was bent over the table beneath the window, clipping sheets of paper together. Her eyes flicked to the briefcase propped against the table-leg. He must have fetched it in from the car. Very early this morning, or late last night? Hadn't he been able to sleep, either?

She loved him so much, her heart felt as if it would burst with the aching pressure of it. And there could be no relief from the awful pain. Her love for him had to be her sad secret.

'There's breakfast if you want it,' he said coolly, pushing the papers into the briefcase and snapping it shut. 'Help yourself.'

Striving for a semblance of normality, she walked over to the heated trolley. Beneath the covered dishes Room Service had provided enough to feed a small army. From the untouched state of everything, Jed obviously wasn't hungry.

Neither was she.

He turned to face her then. Dressed in narrow dark grey trousers, crisp white shirt and a sober blue silk tie, he looked remote and totally unreachable. His face could have been carved from stone, his mouth compressed in a hard, tight line.

She had never seen him look so drained, so utterly world-weary. She upturned the two cups briskly and poured coffee for them both. He needed something.

But he accepted the china cup and saucer with a slight frown, as if he wasn't too sure what it was, put it down on the table-top and told her, 'I'll go down and settle the bill, then I'll pick up a cab on the street. The suite's yours until midday, and be sure you eat something before you drive back to Netherhaye. You're happy about handling the Jag?'

And if she said she wasn't, would that make any difference to the plans he'd obviously made? She wouldn't put bets on it. She put her own untouched coffee back on the trolley. Ignoring his question, she asked, 'Where are you going?'

'Head office. I'll put in a few days' work and stay at my club.'

He dropped a set of car keys on the table and glanced at his watch. He was leaving. He couldn't wait to get away from her. Was he remembering what she'd said last night? Was he disgusted with himself for allowing things to get that far? The gulf between herself and the man she knew she would always love had never seemed so wide.

She couldn't let him walk away like this. They had to talk, discuss the situation properly. The problem of their ruined marriage and far from happy future had to be resolved. They couldn't continue in this painful limbo.

'Do you think that's wise?'

He gave her a bored look.

'What will Catherine think when I return from my glitzy night of triumph on my own and tell her you've cut our supposed honeymoon short so you can get back to work? She'll expect to see us together, looking deliriously happy, you know she will. It was your idea to keep her fooled.'

That did get his attention. She saw his straight brows pull down in a frown and knew he'd registered the implications of what she'd said. She picked up her cup and carried it over to one of the white leather-upholstered armchairs.

'You didn't find your own bunking off a problem,' he reminded her tersely.

'That was entirely different. Even you must see that.' She crossed her long legs at the ankles, took a sip of coffee and tried to keep calm. His bag was already packed, she noticed, ready and waiting by the main door to the suite. 'She's a woman. She knew how important it was—shopping for the perfect dress. She couldn't wait to see every last purchase I'd made. She won't see your ''bunking off'' in quite the same light.'

'Then what do you suggest?' he snapped through his teeth, and pushed his hands into his trouser pockets, his feet planted apart. He looked about as moveable as a mountain, and she narrowed her eyes at him. Why did she love him so very much? He was arrogant, intransigent, stubborn...!

'Nothing at all.' Elena held his coldly bitter eyes. 'I'm not suggesting anything, just demonstrating how impossible this situation is. For both of us. You made a stupid decision and forced it on me. There's no way we can play happy couples for Catherine's benefit and still stay sane.'

He seemed to be weighing up her words. Long seconds passed before he spoke, and then he said slowly, almost silkily, 'You appeared to be happy enough with my proud, adoring husband act yesterday evening, in front of all those people.'

Elena closed her eyes briefly as that taunt sank in. She knew he'd been putting on an act, of course she did, so why did his admission that he was neither proud nor adoring hurt this badly?

Because she was a fool! A fool for hoping in her heart of hearts that he might still feel something for her, just a small echo of his former love.

'And ecstatic, I would imagine,' he went on coldly, 'to discover you could still bring me to my knees with wanting you.'

He gave her a hard look as her face crawled with colour. 'Don't fret about it. I deserved the lesson. I should have known better. A few days ago you "let slip"—' his mouth curled derisively '—that you still loved me. At the time I wondered what your twisted mind was plotting. I stopped believing in your love when I learned of your pregnancy. And last night you let me have the truth right between the eyes. You don't love me, and you never did.' He shot another impatient look at his watch. 'I have to go. And before you start accusing me of cowardice, I do have an important meeting in half an hour.'

At her quick frown he drawled, 'Check with my secretary if you don't believe me. I phoned in yesterday afternoon and heard that a gem dealer from Amsterdam is in town. I got her to set up a meeting. A deal with him, provided the terms are right, would be important enough to convince even Catherine that I needed to break into my wonderful honeymoon. I'll get in touch with Simms and he can pick me up when I'm ready to go back to Netherhaye.'

He was already at the door, on his way, but he told her in the same breath, 'As you appear to be—amazingly—worried about living a lie, I'll give you something to think about. I refuse to lie to Catherine about the true parentage of her coming grandchild. Sam was her whole world, so she'll be delighted to know she'll be able to hold his child one day. So who's going to break the news? And how do we square that within the framework of our blissful marriage? Because that is what it will appear to be on the surface—not for your sake, and God knows not for mine. But for hers, and the child's.'

He looked at her with withering scorn. 'A tough one, isn't it? I think I'll leave it all to you. With your devious mind you should be able to come up with something to convince her!'

She'd had enough—taken too much! She knew her pregnancy had hurt him, and her heart bled for him. But, dammit, he wouldn't believe her side of the story—just closed his mind to everything but hatred!

Colour flamed on her face, and he was part-way out

of the door when she grated at him, 'I'll tell her the truth. It will be a relief to speak to someone who'll do me the courtesy of really listening and believing me, because you darn well won't. If you had ever loved me you would!'

And she fled into her room, locking the door, flinging herself face-down on the bed, taking her rage, frustration and pain out on the pillows. She heard him knocking but shrieked at him to go away, and eventually he must have done, because when she finally pulled herself together the suite was achingly silent.

Drained of all emotion now, she sluiced her face in the bathroom and tied back her hair. She looked at herself in the mirror and saw defeat.

He had the truth, but he couldn't or wouldn't believe it. Her pregnancy meant he didn't want to.

Quickly, before she could sink herself in a mire of misery, she checked her room. Time to go.

She wasn't looking forward to the drive. City streets were a nightmare, the roads out of town would probably be crowded, and she'd never driven anything so powerful as that Jaguar.

And the thought of having to act all bright-eyed and bushy-tailed for her mother-in-law's benefit when she finally made it back to Netherhaye made her feel positively ill.

Her mouth firmed. She had to get a grip. Stop being such a wimp. It wasn't like her to get hysterical, throw childish tantrums, lose all her backbone. She thought of Jed, sitting in that meeting, negotiating yet another dazzling deal, putting her out of his mind quite easily because why think about his devious tramp of a wife when he didn't actually have to?

It helped. If he could block her out and get on with his life then she could do the same.

Picking up her bag, she went through to the sitting room to collect the car keys, and Jed, sprawled out in one of the armchairs, drawled, 'Tantrum over?'

Elena felt as if she was coming unstitched. Just when she thought she'd got herself together again, he popped up and undid all her work. She swallowed thickly. 'You'll be late for your precious meeting.'

'I've rescheduled it for this evening—a working dinner.' He shrugged impressively broad shoulders and hauled himself to his feet. He took her overnight bag and told her, 'I never knew you could get hysterical if you didn't get your own way. One of the joys of being newly wed? Learning something different about one's partner every day?'

She hated it when he was sarcastic. It made her hurt so badly she couldn't think of a snappy come-back, and simply stared at him when he said, 'I'll take you home, then drive back in for that meeting. Shall we go?'

'There's no need. I'm—'

'The state you're in, do you think I'd have a moment's peace if you were behind the wheel of a potentially lethal weapon?'

He held the door open for her and all she could do was follow. She'd been perfectly capable of driving— if not exactly looking forward to the city traffic—before he'd popped up where she hadn't expected him to be and ruined everything.

She didn't suppose he'd altered his arrangement out of concern for her well-being. He wouldn't have a moment's peace if he thought she was likely to put a dent in his prestigious car!

As he held the passenger door open for her five minutes later he gave her a narrow-eyed stare. 'When we've cleared the traffic you can tell me more about this story you've concocted to convince Catherine that you and I can live happily ever after, despite the little hiccup of your being pregnant with my brother's child. Fasten your seat belt.'

He closed the door and paced round the front of the gleaming silver car. She closed her eyes defeatedly.

Of course he didn't believe her. Had she really expected he would? There was too much going on inside his head as far as Sam was concerned to let him accept the truth.

The silence between them was intense, building up to scary proportions as the sleek car edged forward in the inevitable traffic snarl-ups. Jed's long fingers drummed impotently on the steering wheel, his profile grim. Despite the warmth of the early summer day Elena shivered. She couldn't wait until they got out of this and hit the open road. Maybe then this twisting tension would ease off just a little, allow her racing heartbeats to settle down.

But when they did she wished they hadn't, because he said, 'Congratulations. When you came up with this fairy tale—nothing between you and Sam but a clinical procedure—I thought it was to placate me. But it wasn't, was it? It was a way of getting Catherine on your side. Our marriage ends in divorce—which is what you want—you come out of it smelling of roses and I'm the big, bad ogre. Bully for you! Who else but you could have come up with such a story? It's too incredible not to be believed.'

'Except by you, of course,' she said through her teeth, staring out of the window at her side, uninterestedly watching the stockbroker belt slip by.

'Of course,' he concurred, uncharacteristically slowing down a touch to keep within the speed limit. Elena gave a mental shrug. She had expected him to really put his foot down, deliver her back to Netherhaye in record time, not prolong the agony of being cocooned here together, physically close but mentally and emotionally at opposite ends of the galaxy.

'Whether you believe it or not, it's the truth,' she told him bitterly.

Jed gave a derisive snort. 'Lady, you slay me! Do you actually believe I'm green enough to fall for such an unlikely story? For starters,' he bit out, when her only answer was a weary shrug, 'if it had been the truth you'd have told me about it.'

Stung into speech by the unfairness of that, she retorted, 'I tried to, remember? Several times. You flatly refused to listen. Then, when you had no option but to listen, you decided I was telling lies. You decided Sam and I had been having an affair and I'd married you knowing I was carrying his child.'

'I mean *before* we married. You didn't think to warn me we might be expecting the patter of tiny feet rather sooner than I might have expected.'

She let her head sag back against the smooth leather upholstery. She felt too wretched to speak. And what was the point in telling him anything? He would only accuse her of lying, whatever she said.

'Well?' he prompted coolly. 'I do need to know, if

you intend to spin this yarn for Catherine. We need to get our stories straight.'

Elena's stomach knotted painfully. How could something that had been so beautiful have come to this? The death of love was a terrible, terrible thing. Couldn't he see what tying them together with lies created for public consumption would do to them?

Outside the car the rolling countryside shimmered in the early summer heat; inside the air-conditioning made her shiver—or perhaps it was the icy wash of his voice. 'If anyone asks I take it you intend to say I was fully aware of the situation all along? The truth—that I was completely in the dark until circumstances forced you to come clean—would point to a certain lack of common decency on your part.'

'Accuse me of anything you like,' she said thickly, pain tearing through her, 'but not a lack of decency.'

She had made her decision not to tell him of what she and Sam had arranged until Jed had done his grieving for his brother. It might have been the wrong decision, but it had been made with the best of intentions.

She turned wretched eyes in his direction, then quickly looked away. The grim contempt on his hard profile was unbearable. 'On the day of Sam's funeral I started what I thought was a period and truly believed the treatment hadn't worked,' she whispered threadily. 'Somehow, it made the sadness even worse. Over the years of our friendship he and I discussed many things—marriage and children amongst them. I longed for a child,' she confessed. 'But I'd had one taste of marriage and didn't want a second. Sam said he wouldn't marry because of the nature of his work, but he regretted not having a child because he believed that having a child was the only claim to immortality the human race could hope for.'

Talking about it now, she couldn't hold the words back. They tumbled over each other, urgent, low, probably too low for him to hear everything she said. That wasn't really important now, because he wouldn't believe her in any case, but verbalising her memories gave her a tiny measure of reassurance.

'We decided, for our own separate reasons, to try to make a baby. Sam had a friend in London—head of a private clinic—and pulled in a favour. But, like I said, I thought the treatment hadn't worked. Looking at his grave that day, I knew he'd lost his claim to immortality, as he'd seen it. It added a heavier burden of sadness. I wasn't prepared to put that on you at that time. I truly thought it best to wait.'

She leaned her head sideways on the back of the seat, staring through the window. Jed's silence was like a heavy weight. Had he heard what she'd said? Was he sifting through it, looking for something he could use to prove she lied? Or did he consider the whole unlikely story unworthy of comment?

The latter, most probably, she decided with a wretchedly miserable mental shrug. There seemed no point in asking him. She was too emotionally drained to counter any further scornful accusations.

Another fifteen minutes would see them back at Netherhaye. Would the gods be kind? Would Catherine be in the cottage garden, making plans to transform it when she and Susan took up residence? Or would she be home, waiting to hear every last detail of last night's ceremony, fully expecting her to be bubbling with happiness and excitement?

The thought of being plunged into pretending life was a ball, without a breathing space to get herself together, drained her already meagre supply of energy.

To take her mind off the prospect, and Jed's continuing telling silence, she forced herself to concentrate on the passing scenery.

The lanes were narrower now, the verges a tangle of Queen Anne's Lace, wild roses and honeysuckle, the overhanging trees heavy with new leaf. And every time her eyes dropped to the wing mirror she saw the dusty blue Escort that she was sure she'd seen close behind them way back in the city streets.

It was unlikely to be the same car, of course. That make was very common. But watching it, sometimes left behind as the Jaguar swept round a bend, sometimes coming up close, then dropping back to a safe distance, gave her something other than misery to occupy her mind.

When the Jaguar turned off into Netherhaye's long, tree-lined drive the blue car went straight on towards the village, and all Elena's dread of having to face Catherine and pretend came flooding back. But Jed cut the engine well before the house came into sight.

He turned to her in the green silence and softly put his hand over hers. She lifted bewildered eyes to him, his touch riveting her to her seat. She was incapable of movement. Whatever she'd expected, it wasn't tenderness. It altered everything. Instinctively, her fingers wound around his, his touch making her breathless.

He'd been looking at their entwined hands, and now he raised his eyes to lock with hers. She thought she saw a longing there in the smoky depths, some deep emotion that echoed the longing in her heart.

She trembled, tears shimmering in her eyes, and he held her hand more tightly, just for a moment, then pulled away, gripping the steering wheel, his knuckles showing white.

'Elena—can we cool it?' he asked flatly. 'Give it more time—give me more time?' His eyes swept her troubled face. 'I'd like to think I did—do—mean something to you. It's tough knowing what to believe, given the circumstances, but I'm working on it. The whole situation's done my head in, and believe me, that's not something I'm happy with. Will you give me more time to get to grips with this before you go along a path we'd both find difficult to retrace?'

She dipped her head in silent acknowledgement of his words, biting down hard on her lower lip, sucking it between her teeth, holding back dredging disappointment.

Stupid to have hoped he was ready to say he believed what she'd told him, was willing to go forward, build on the rebirth of trust and understanding.

Had he asked for more time just to stop her walking away? Making the breakdown of their marriage public, shattering Catherine's happy illusions and making it difficult for him to have a say in his brother's child's future welfare—much less be the constant presence in his or her life he had always insisted on?

Or had he really had a change of heart? Had he been telling the truth when he'd implied he was trying to come to terms with everything that had happened, that he wanted to be able to believe she loved him?

She didn't know. But she had to take the chance because it was the only one she had.

'I'll go along with that. Take all the time you need. I want you to believe me because, God knows, it's the truth,' she told him falteringly, and hoped to heaven she was doing the right thing in letting herself hope, not storing up more pain for the future, handing him a sharpened stake to thrust through her already bleeding heart.

CHAPTER NINE

RELUCTANTLY, Elena left the rustic seat at the far end of the garden, the one with the view over miles of open countryside, and began to amble slowly back towards the house.

She treasured these early-morning walks and the solitude she found; it was her way of escaping for just a little while. During the three days of Jed's absence his mother had done nothing but chatter. She'd wanted to know every last detail of the ceremony, had clipped out every newspaper report she could find and was proudly sticking them in a scrapbook. And when that subject was temporarily exhausted she chattered excitedly about the cottage, the changes she and Susan would make after they moved in.

It was perfectly understandable. Talking non-stop about everything and anything took her mind off the recent loss of her son, and Elena was more than happy to listen, but she did need a few quiet times of her own in which to do some thinking.

Jed had phoned each evening. Until last night they'd been duty calls, largely made, Elena suspected, for his mother's benefit, nothing personal.

But that had changed last night, when he'd said, 'I've thought a lot about what you told me and there's more I want to ask. But I'm beginning to think we can work this out—if you want that. I'll be home tomorrow evening, hopefully around dinner time?

Perhaps we should go back to Las Rocas. What do you think? We need to talk some more, and we can do it more easily on our own.'

Hope had lapped her body with warmth as she'd agreed shakily, a little breathlessly. 'That sounds fine.' And it had. It couldn't get much finer. At least now he was willing to talk, perhaps to believe her and begin to understand the desperate, gnawing need that had driven her to accept Sam's offer. 'Shall I book the flights?'

'No, leave it to me. I'll arrange it for Friday, if I can.'

She had said, because it had been bothering her, 'I really do think Catherine should be told about the baby before we leave. I couldn't fasten my jeans this morning, so by the time we come back from Spain—' fingers crossed they would be coming back together '—it might be obvious. I've no idea how quickly these things happen.'

His ensuing silence had alarmed her. Had it been too soon, taking too much for granted, to talk about her pregnancy with such apparent ease? It was a subject he couldn't be happy with, and she could understand that. But the need to tell Catherine the truth had been playing on her mind.

'You're quite right,' he'd agreed at last. 'Whatever happens, she has to know the truth. Would you prefer to break the news on your own, or would you rather wait until I can be there?'

'On my own, I think.' The way he'd said 'whatever happens' meant he wasn't sure about their future at all, she'd recognised dispiritedly. She didn't want any bad vibes coming from him to spoil whatever pleasure

Catherine could take in knowing her beloved Sam had left a child.

And now she was going back to the house to find Catherine and have that talk. Elena's mouth went dry at the prospect. Unconsciously she straightened her shoulders, and tucked her workmanlike blue and white striped shirt more firmly beneath the waistband of her loosely styled white cotton chinos.

She ran Catherine to earth in the morning room, making designs for her new garden on graph paper. 'Darling! You were quick—did you get everything you needed?'

'I haven't been to the village yet.' Elena wandered over to the window seat where Catherine was working. 'I've been having a lazy walk around the garden.' And thinking about what I have to tell you, and how I'll tell it, and wondering how you're going to take it, she added silently.

'Oh—if I'd known!' Catherine transferred the block of graph paper from her knees to a small coffee table at her side. 'When he phoned I couldn't find you, and Edith said she hadn't seen you, so we thought you'd already gone to the village.'

'Who phoned?' Elena sat on the other end of the window seat, trying not to let her sudden panic show.

Jed? Had he changed his mind about coming home this evening? About Spain? Had he decided they had nothing to talk about after all?

'A journalist from one of the women's magazines— I quite forget which one. They want to do an interview with you,' Catherine answered excitedly. 'About your books, and the award, and whether you'll be making your home here or dividing your time between here and Las Rocas. He seemed really keen for information. If I'd known you were only in the garden I would have come to fetch you. Anyway, he said he'd phone back later on to arrange an appointment, so I'm sure he will—as I said, he seemed very keen—so many questions!'

Elena's smile was one of relief. Her panic attack had been for nothing, except, of course, to show her how very much she was hoping she and Jed could find a way through this mess.

She dismissed the journalist and his interview easily from her mind. She supposed she should be flattered, or interested, but she wasn't. There were far more important things in life. 'Catherine,' she said gently. 'I have something to tell you.'

Choosing her words with care, she began at the beginning, watching Catherine's eyes grow wider with every word she said, then filming with tears as she whispered, 'Sam's baby—I can't tell you how much that means to me. To hold a child of his in my arms, a living part of him. And I can understand why you agreed to it at that time. I don't think men can properly understand the primeval instinct to mother—I guess you felt your biological clock ticking away and panicked.

'And typical of Sam, too, bless him! He always said life was too short to miss out on the things you really wanted, and if the opportunity arose you upped and grabbed it. Much as I loved him, I'm afraid that the words "duty" and "responsibility" were a foreign language to him. Though what he lacked in that department, Jed more than made up for. And—' Her teeth worried at her lower lip. 'What was Jed's reaction?'

'He wasn't exactly ecstatic,' Elena understated. 'But I promise you, he's working on it.' It was as much as she could offer. It would be cruel to paint a rosy picture when everything could still go badly wrong.

'Yes,' Catherine remarked softly. 'Jed would work hard to accept it. He's such a strong character and I know how very much he loves you. He told me he found the missing half of himself when he found you.' She put her fingertips to her suddenly trembling mouth. 'I do hope the poor boy doesn't feel he's lost out to Sam again. That would be unbearable for him.'

'Lost out again?' Elena questioned gently, her pulses quickening. Was Catherine about to confirm what she already suspected—that for some unfathomable reason Jed felt he came a poor second-best to his matinée-idol-handsome younger brother? 'How could that possibly be?'

'It's entirely my fault; I know that.' Catherine answered the question in her inimitable, round-about-the-houses way, her eyes anxious. 'I feel so guilty when I think about it all. At the time we thought we were doing the right thing. Park House is such an excellent prep school, and it had been arranged that Jed should go there when he was eight.

'Sam was just a tiny baby then—a sickly baby, demanding all my attention. I absolutely refused to hire a nanny; I needed to care for him myself. From one or two things Jed let slip when he was in his early teens I'm sure, with hindsight, he must have felt he'd been pushed out—especially when Sam wasn't sent away to school but was tutored privately at home. He was still a frail little boy, and wayward and wilful, too. We knew he wouldn't fit in with school discipline.'

She was twisting her fingers together so frenziedly that Elena thought her mother-in-law's hands might fall apart at any moment. She took one of them in hers and held it gently. She couldn't believe this warm and loving woman would ever knowingly hurt anyone. 'I'm sure you did what you thought best.'

'I didn't think about it deeply enough!' Catherine castigated herself, her fingers gripping Elena's now. 'Because Jed was always stronger and tougher than his brother, in every possible way, it was Sam who got the lion's share of encouragement and cosseting. And because we knew the family business would be safe in Jed's hands it was Sam who got to do what he wanted in life.

'Jed was never asked what he wanted; we just took it for granted he'd do his duty and shoulder the responsibility. And after his father died Jed was always here for me—strong, supportive, clear-headed and caring. While Sam—well, we often didn't know where he was for weeks and months at a time.

'So when he did come home for a few days between assignments what did I do? The prodigal son and fatted calf wasn't in it! The silly thing is, I think—no, I *know*—that I made much more fuss of Sam to make up for secretly loving Jed the best.'

Elena gently released her hand from Catherine's clutching fingers. What she'd said explained so much, why the fact that it was Sam's child she was carrying had been so hard for Jed to face, for starters. Hadn't she asked him to try to imagine if his reaction would have been the same if she'd had a brief affair with any other man and fallen pregnant, well before she'd even met him?

He wouldn't have been delighted, but because he was a highly intelligent, compassionate man, without, until recently, a jealous bone in his body, he would have understood that mistakes can happen. And, because they'd loved each other, he would have found a way to accept it.

But because *Sam* was her child's father he simply couldn't take it. Even if the baby's conception had been the result of clinical treatment.

She said quietly, 'Thank you for telling me this. I think you should tell Jed, too. Explain it, as you've just explained it to me. It would wipe away his misconceptions about coming a poor second-best to his brother.'

She stood up, finding a reassuring smile. 'I'll make some coffee; we could both do with some. And don't worry. You did a fine job of bringing up both your boys. Sam was clever, charming, a great friend to many people, and he excelled in the work he did; he took it very seriously. And Jed—' She spread her hands expressively. 'Jed is simply the best.'

Elena got back from her delayed trip to the village at a little after three o'clock that afternoon, just as the phone rang. She put the packages and carriers she'd brought in from the car down on the parquet floor of the hall and lifted the receiver, pushing her hair out of her eyes with her free hand.

If it was the journalist who'd called earlier he'd be wasting his time. She and Jed would be on their way back to Spain by this time tomorrow.

It wasn't. It was Liam. Elena took the instrument from her ear and stared at it, frowning. She couldn't believe it. Why would her ex-husband be calling her? How did he know she was here?

His insistent voice on the other end of the line had her reluctantly listening again, her soft mouth pulled down in distaste.

'What do you want?' she asked him frigidly, wondering if he'd bother to phone again if she simply put the receiver down and cut him off.

'I just told you.'

'And I wasn't listening,' she told him back.

'Then you'd better listen this time,' he said toughly. 'I want money. Big fat bunches of the stuff. And I want it now. Because of you I was banged up. You turned me in. I always treated you right, showed you a good time,' he said resentfully. 'Now I've paid my debt to society,' he sneered. 'So it's your turn to clear your debt to me.'

'I don't owe you a single thing.' She couldn't believe she was hearing this. It was surreal.

'Ten years at Her Majesty's pleasure. You call that nothing? You set me up. You owe me. And don't tell me you can't afford it. I know better. And don't say you won't, because if you do I'll make big, big trouble. For you and your nice new husband.'

Elena's eyes flicked round the hall. The house felt empty, but she knew it wasn't. At any minute Catherine might wander through and want to know if she was talking to that nice journalist who had phoned earlier.

How could she explain that she wasn't, that she was

speaking to her ex-husband, the ex-convict, who was now demanding money with menaces?

She really could do without this on top of everything else!

Dealing with it firmly, she said, 'Get lost. You're talking nonsense.'

'OK. If that's the way you want it. You just sit back and wait till the rubbish hits the fan. You and hubby will be covered with it.'

Her stomach contracted and goosebumps peaked on her skin. He sounded as if he really meant it, as if he had some dirt he was waiting to fling over her and Jed.

She couldn't think what. He was the one who had plenty to hide. Nevertheless, it had to be dealt with. She didn't want him even trying to make trouble. She and Jed already had enough of that on their hands.

'We can't talk here,' she said with sharp aggravation. Talking to him at all was the last thing she wanted, but she had to find out what was on his sneaky mind so she could do something about it.

'Now you're being sensible, babe.'

There'd been a time when his slight cockney accent had fascinated her. Now she felt nothing. 'So give me your number and I'll call you back,' she instructed coldly. She'd have to drive back to the village and use the public call box. She could make the excuse that she'd forgotten something. It was a damned nuisance, because she'd meant to spend what was left of the afternoon making herself look good for Jed, planning what she'd say to him.

She scrabbled around in the drawer of the table for paper and something to write with, but he derided,

'You think I'm stupid, or something? Meet me at the end of hubby's fancy drive in fifteen minutes.'

So he was close. That close?

For the first time she felt scared. When she'd married him all those years ago she'd thought she knew him. One year on she'd discovered she hadn't known him at all. Who knew what evil retaliation he had in his mind?

She glanced at her watch. No way would she let him know he was beginning to worry her. 'Make it an hour,' she said firmly, and tried not to shake.

'Why? So you can call in the cavalry?'

'No, because it suits me.'

She replaced the receiver decisively and leant against the table, waiting for her heartbeats to steady. In one hour's time Catherine would be resting in her room, something she always did because, as she said, she was sixty years old and entitled to pamper herself.

And Edith would have come over from the converted stable-block she and her husband had occupied for years to begin preparing the special dinner they'd planned to welcome Jed home.

Dinner was always at eight at Netherhaye, so Jed was unlikely to be arriving before seven. 'Around dinner time,' he'd said.

That gave her plenty of time to get rid of Liam and make sure he didn't come back.

Exactly one hour later her confidence had haemorrhaged away, and the winding, tree-lined drive seemed endless, her legs feeling uncomfortably shaky, as if they might give way under her at any moment.

Liam Forrester's pleasure was Liam Forrester's

main preoccupation. He liked to have a good time, liked fast cars, high living, was happy to cheat and steal to get what he wanted. Being behind bars would not have made him a happy man.

And her evidence had put him there.

As Liam stepped out from beneath the trees she suppressed a cry of alarm. She refused to let him see any sign of fear.

He swept his eyes over her casually clothed body, making her skin crawl. 'You could do with a bit of glitz, and I'd never let you wear trousers—you've got fabulous legs. But you look good. Success suits you.'

Prison hadn't suited him. It was almost a shock to see how he'd altered. His blond hair had dulled to an ashy brown and looked unkempt, he'd grown a paunch, and the once sharp dresser was now wearing stained, shabby black trousers and a cheap imitation leather jacket.

'How did you know where I was?'

The question was forced from her. Her life when she'd been married to him seemed so long ago. He was the part of her past she'd wanted to expunge from her memory; she had almost forgotten his existence.

'Easy. I've been following your career with interest. Not much else to do in the nick but read the papers. And plan how I'd catch up with you one day and see you shared your success with me—like I shared mine with you once upon a time. Trouble was, I read you lived somewhere in Spain, so when I got out I couldn't get my hands on you.'

He stepped closer. He'd put on weight and looked big and threatening. The lane that passed the end of the drive was rarely used. Anything could happen.

He saw the fear in her eyes and smiled. 'Don't worry, I'm not daft enough to wring the neck of the golden goose! I reckon fate's on my side for once. It was a stroke of luck seeing that piece in the paper about you winning that award. I just needed to hang around, follow you down here, book into the village pub and ask a few questions.'

The blue Escort, she thought tiredly. And questions. 'You phoned earlier pretending to be a journalist,' she stated.

He grinned, and for the first time she caught a fleeting echo of the good-looking, easy-on-the-eye charmer he had been when she'd first met him.

All her girlfriends had been deeply envious of the way he'd pursued her so single-mindedly. If only they had known what he really was they would have pitied her instead. If only she hadn't been so flattered, so dazzled, naively incapable of seeing the real man behind the façade.

'Talkative woman, your mother-in-law. I even got the address of your Spanish home,' he boasted. 'I quite fancy lazing around on a Costa, drinking sangria in the sun, but for the time being ten thou will do. In cash. Tomorrow. Same time, same place. Or else.'

She glared at him, appalled. There had to be a way out of this nightmare, she thought wildly. The police? If she took out an injunction to make him stay away from her would that apply in Spain, or would she also have to go through the Spanish courts?

Jed, she thought weakly. Oh, if only he were here! He would know what to do.

She swung on her heels, heading back for the house. Liam was out of his head if he thought she'd hand over that kind of money and then sit back and wait until he came and asked for more!

If he'd shown some remorse for his crimes, said he was on his uppers and trying to go straight, then she would have gladly given him something to help him get on his feet again and find honest work. But this— this was extortion with menaces! He would never change.

'Don't walk away from me!' His hand grabbed her arm before she'd gone two paces. There was brutal violence in his voice now and she stood very still, hardly daring to breathe. She couldn't bear him touching her, wanted to shake him off, but didn't dare provoke him.

'That's better.' He sounded calmer now, and he said with a honeyed sweetness that sent shivers down her spine, 'I can spin a good yarn, too, honeybunch. You don't have a monopoly. It would be a real cracker in the hands of a top journalist. Given the type of publicity you get, the tabloids would pay well for the skeleton in your cupboard. Married to a common criminal, enjoying all the goodies—which of your readers is going to believe you didn't have a part in it? Or at the very least know what was going on, where all that extra money was coming from, and fully condone it?

'Dirt sticks, sweetie-pie. It would cause a small sensation, but just imagine what it could do if the more sober broadsheets picked it up.' His fingers tightened on her arm as he bent and whispered in her ear. 'Your husband's an establishment guy; he heads an awesome establishment-type business. The customers for his fabulous gems come from the very top social drawer. There's many a royal lady wearing something fabulous from Nolan's. Bit of a slur on the revered family name to have it coupled with a woman with that kind of past, wouldn't you say?

'The nobs just might start buying their platinum and diamond knick-knacks from one or other of his high-falutin' rivals.' He jerked her closer. 'So pay up, or, as I said—take the consequences.'

He pulled her even closer, intimately close. And she could do nothing about it. All the stuffing had been knocked out of her. He meant it, all of it. He'd get the money one way or another.

In the light of the publicity surrounding her recent acceptance of that prestigious award the seamier tabloids would pay top dollar for his story, his warped allegations, disregarding the fact that there might not be any truth in them because stuff like that sold papers.

People liked to see other people get to the top, but they liked it better when they saw them knocked right back down again!

She could handle it for herself, but she couldn't let Jed and the Nolan gem empire be smothered in that kind of slimy publicity. She couldn't let that happen to him.

'You can have your money,' she said bitterly, hating having to give way but having no choice. 'I don't have that amount in my UK account. But we're going back to Spain tomorrow. I can get my hands on it there and send—'

'I'll give you three days.' He stuck his face inches from hers. 'And I'll come to Spain and pick it up in person. No cheques in the post, nothing traceable. Cash. I know where to find you, remember.' He pushed his face closer. 'Is your phone unlisted?'

She shook her head, trying to draw back. He wouldn't let her.

'Good. I'll call you. Tell you when and where to meet me.'

The scrunch of tyres on the gravelled surface of the drive had Liam pulling his face out of hers, turning his head. Elena felt weak with relief. Being so close to him had made her feel nauseous and dizzy. But she would rather collapse in a heap than cling onto the foul blackmailer. Only when she heard the expensive clunk of the Jaguar's door did she fully understand what was happening.

Frantically forcing her brain to function, she turned. Jed had returned hours earlier than expected. She didn't know whether to be glad or sorry.

Sorry, she supposed sinkingly, as she looked into his hard, expressionless face. Wearing the dark grey trousers of a business suit, his white shirt tie-less, open at the neck, sleeves rolled up to the elbow, he looked gorgeous. But quelling.

'I guess you must be husband Mark Two.' It was Liam who broke the heavy silence. He advanced, cast an appreciative eye over the gleaming car, extended his hand, which Jed ignored, and aimed for a clipped public school accent but failed. 'I'm Mark One. For your sake, old boy, I hope she doesn't do the dirty on you like she did on me. But don't put money on it.'

His hand dropped back to his side. 'Well, if you're not going to invite me in for drinkies, I'll be on my way.' He shrugged, stuffed both hands in the pockets of his disreputable trousers and swaggered away. Then he turned, his smile malicious. 'Take a tip from me, old boy. With that woman around you'd better learn to watch your back.'

CHAPTER TEN

'WHAT was he doing here?'

Jed looked at her with narrowed eyes. The afternoon sun was hot, but Elena shivered. He was looking at her with cold suspicion when she'd wanted to see the beginnings of the trust and understanding he'd hinted at in last night's telephone conversation.

Liam had ruined his homecoming.

'Asking for hand-outs,' she told him, setting her jaw, because if she let herself relax her teeth would start to rattle with nervous tension. She knew she couldn't tell him the whole truth about her ex-husband's successful blackmail attempt because Jed would insist on calling his bluff, contacting the police, and then those smears and allegations would end up in the tabloids. She couldn't let that happen.

It might, as Liam had threatened, actually harm his business, not to mention his reputation, and even if it didn't, seeing his wife's name smeared in the gutter press would hurt his pride. He'd take it on the chin, but he'd find it deeply distasteful.

'What for?' he asked tightly. 'The price of a pint? New clothes—he looked as if he could use them! Or more? Was it more, Elena?'

'Of course.' She hadn't been able to keep the bitterness out of her voice. She could have said, Just something to tide him over while he looks for work—something to take the steam out of the situation. But she hated having to lie to Jed, even by leaving things unsaid.

He caught her tone. Of course he did. 'And did you give it to him? The way you were folded round each other when I turned into the drive suggests you might have done. He looked remarkably pleased with himself, and you looked as if you weren't averse to reliving old times.'

From his viewpoint it could have looked that way. She had to give him that, she conceded miserably. Yet she couldn't tell him what had really been happening. She shuffled her feet in the gravel, realised what she was doing, how guilty and embarrassed the childish action would make her look, and stopped, pushed her hands into the pockets of her trousers and shrugged.

'Hardly that. Old times with Liam are something I'd prefer to forget. I certainly wouldn't want to relive a second of them. And how could I give him anything, even if I'd wanted to? I've only got pin money with me, and I couldn't write a cheque because my UK account is as good as empty.'

She'd only kept it going because it had been handy to have something to draw on when she visited the UK for meetings with her agent and publisher. Since coming over for Sam's funeral and her wedding, and now the awards, she'd practically cleaned it out.

He seemed to accept that, but probed ruthlessly, 'Did you tell him where to find you?'

'Of course not!' Did he think she'd kept in touch with Liam, perhaps even met up with him after his release from prison? That made her very angry. How could he think she'd do that and, worse, keep it from him?

He acknowledged her flare of anger with a dip of his head, his narrowed eyes not leaving her face, as if he was looking for the truth and couldn't find it. 'Then I'm to take it that his appearance at Netherhaye was a wondrous coincidence, an unlooked-for opportunity on his part to ask you for money,' he said, with a dryness that set her teeth on edge.

By the way her skin was burning she knew her face had turned brick-red. Fury, frustration and resentment coiled her insides into a tight knot. Just when she and Jed might have had a chance to work through their problems and find each other again, when he might have learned to love and trust her once more, Liam had swaggered along and driven an even bigger wedge between them.

'Can't we forget the creep?' she asked impulsively. 'I had nothing at all to do with him being here. He followed us down, apparently. He'd read about the award ceremony and thought I'd be a soft touch. He phoned earlier and suggested we meet. Believe me, I didn't want to, but I agreed because I didn't want him hanging around, making a nuisance of himself.'

She couldn't tell him any more. She hoped to heaven what she had told him would be enough, that he'd put the whole nasty episode out of his mind. And it seemed her prayers had been answered, because he opened the car on the passenger side and held the door for her. 'Get in. You might as well ride up to the house with me.'

And when he joined her and turned on the ignition his tone was the same, cool and distant. 'I take it Catherine's having her afternoon nap? Ask Edith to bring a tray of tea out onto the terrace, would you? I could do with a reviver before I shower.'

That careful politeness set the tone for the remainder of the afternoon and evening. It was as if, she thought as she tried to do justice to Edith's delicious marinated salmon steaks, served with baby new potatoes fresh from the garden and spicy ratatouille, his mind was functioning smoothly on the surface while sorting through the ramifications of the scene he'd come upon with her and Liam.

She risked a look at him as she sipped her iced spring water. He looked so darned controlled. Too controlled? Would his emotions burst through, blowing them both away?

'Now, neither of you must worry about me,' Catherine said when Edith had cleared the used plates and dishes. Jed had already told her they'd be leaving early next morning to catch the flight to Jerez—told her in that same calm, dispassionate voice. 'I expect Susan to arrive any day. Apparently she's a knock-out on the sewing machine—so we'll measure up for curtains, take a trip into town and choose the fabric. We're going to be so busy! So make the most of the rest of your honeymoon and don't give me a second thought.'

'Talking of which, I'll go and sort out the documents dealing with the lease on the property in Seville.' Jed turned his soulless smile on Catherine. 'And, no, I won't spend most of the time working.' He declined the fresh strawberries and helped himself to coffee, taking it with him, and Elena knew it was an excuse to leave them, to do his thinking without having to make polite conversation.

'I haven't had a chance to say anything to him about the baby,' Catherine confessed mournfully, helping herself to the berries. 'I did try to start a conversation before you came down for dinner, lead up to it gently, but he put on that remote face and froze me off.' She put down her spoon. 'I'm worried about him, Elena.'

'Don't be.' Said with more confidence than she felt. 'I get the feeling Jed can cope with anything life throws at him.' Her certainty of that went bone-deep. But after the scene with Liam would his form of coping revert to what it had been? The total blanking off, cutting her out of his heart with surgical precision?

She didn't think she could bear that, not after being so sure he was on the point of breaking through to an understanding of the events that had led to her pregnancy, and through that understanding learning to forgive her—and Sam.

Liam had done more harm than he would ever know.

'I can't help worrying, it being Sam's baby—'

'Try not to,' Elena soothed. Suddenly the stresses of the day caught up with her, draining her energy. She wanted to crawl into a hole and hide, and only come out when all the bad things had gone away. 'You'll have your chance to talk to him—about the baby, and his and his brother's childhood—soon enough. Right now he's working things out for himself. He needs space.' She finished her coffee and pushed herself tiredly to her feet. 'If you don't mind, I think I'll go and pack. I might see you later, if I don't fall asleep first! And if you see Edith before I do, tell her from me the meal was perfect.'

Packing for them both took next to no time. Elena

looked at the big double bed and wondered if Jed would join her. Pointless wondering when in her heart she knew he wouldn't.

If Liam hadn't done so much damage he might have done. Maybe they would have talked far into the night. Or maybe he would have simply held her. Or maybe simply slept at her side, not touching, not talking. That would have been enough.

She put a couple of soft down pillows and a light blanket on the chaise longue and got ready to occupy the bed in solitary state.

It was more of the same the next day. Not until they were in the hire car leaving Jerez airport did a hint of a thaw creep in.

They had the windows down, and she was sure she could smell the sherry on the hot air, the scent so evocative of this wealthy, productive corner of Andalucia. She watched Jed fill his lungs, certain he was beginning to look more approachable, and asked, 'Do you mind if we detour through Cadiz?'

'Sure.' He eased the car into the traffic and headed south. 'We're going to need provisions, I guess. I don't suppose you got around to getting in touch with Pilar to let her know we were coming?'

She hadn't even thought of it. All her mental energies had been focused on him. But his mention of the provisions she had overlooked handed her the excuse she'd been racking her tired brain to find.

'I'll need to go to the bank for cash, and then I thought we could stop by the market.' She clutched at the excuse he had given her gratefully. 'We could either eat out—early-supper-cum-late-lunch—or head straight back to Las Rocas.'

'Head back,' he said. 'I fancy a quiet night in the mountains.' He stamped on the brakes as a yellow Seat, covered in the white dust of the local Albariza soil, cut across them with long, strident blasts of its horn. Jed grinned, his teeth very white against his sun-darkened skin. 'Spanish maniac! Still, I could get used to it!'

She left him parking the car while she went into the Banco de Andalucia. She couldn't have felt more guilty if she'd been wearing a stocking on her head and carrying a sawn-off shotgun. She felt sneaky and devious, doing this behind Jed's back.

But he would have refused to allow her to give in to blackmail demands, and then he would have had to suffer the hateful consequences, she knew that, so even though she felt awful about it she was doing this for his sake, because she loved him. For herself, Liam could have gone ahead and done his worst.

Thankfully, because she was a valued customer and well known at this branch, the transaction was completed swiftly. And she walked out onto the hot pavement with the pay-off for Liam stuffed at the bottom of her handbag and the bunch of pesetas for household expenses innocently folded in her purse.

Jed was strolling towards her, the breeze from the ocean ruffling his soft dark hair. Her heart flipped. He was so special, so very much loved.

She waited for him, watching the way he moved. She loved his grace, his elegant strength. It made her heart hurt; it always had and always would. And the way his eyes lit with warmth when he saw her made her give him a lilting smile. Perhaps she could let herself believe that he'd done his thinking and their time here together would be special and important, a time of coming to terms with what had happened, accepting it and going on together.

And Liam, hopefully, completely out of the frame.

'I should have thought to ask you to wait.' His eyes went to the open doors of the bank. 'I could have changed a few traveller's cheques. Want to come back in with me while I do it?'

Stopping him from going into the bank with her had been precisely why she'd asked him to drop her off while he found somewhere to park. 'No need,' she told him blithely. 'Let's hit the market! I withdrew plenty.' And wasn't that the truth!

'OK. Shopping, if you say so—I'll just try to get used to being a kept man. I keep forgetting I'm married to a wealthy woman!'

His relaxed smile gave her the courage to tuck her arm through his, just companionably, nothing to make him think she was about to repeat the flaunty, flirty behaviour she'd so misguidedly produced when they'd spent the day here with Catherine.

Born out of pain, a primitive need to hurt him back, it hadn't been one of her better ideas.

She was aiming for friendly, not flirty. Friends exploring the busy, colourful market, heads together as they examined the piles of fresh produce for the best bargains, having mild arguments over the choice of swordfish steaks, giant prawns or clams, amicably resolving the difficulty by buying some of each.

When they were overburdened with bags almost bursting with irresistible fruit and vegetables they looked at each other and grinned.

'Whose army are we aiming to feed?' Jed's eyes

were warm, soft silver, his sexy mouth relaxed, smiling for her, and Elena felt herself sliding effortlessly back into the safe haven of his love.

At least, that was what she felt here and now, in the bustle and noise of the exotic outdoor market, with the Spanish sun beating down, and she was going to hang onto the feeling and hope nothing happened to take it away.

'I guess we should make tracks for home and start chomping our way through it.' Aquamarine eyes sparkled for him. 'But how about grabbing an orange juice first?'

'Not only beautiful, but bright too.' He took her share of the bulging carriers and added them to his own. 'Lead on. The rabbit warren of narrow streets confuses me.'

Nothing confused him, Elena thought, keeping up with his long, effortless stride. Present him with a problem and he'd work it out, calmly, intelligently and logically. Which was what he'd done regarding the problem their marriage had faced.

The fire and fury bit at first had been natural. His emotions had got in the way of logic. But he'd had his thinking time and—her heart lifted, spinning wildly—everything was going to be all right! Suddenly she was deliriously sure of it.

They found a restaurant on the Plaza Topete, and, sitting at a table on the *terraza*, surrounded by urns brimming with perfumed flowers, sipping huge glasses of freshly squeezed orange juice, Jed remarked, 'I take it the creep was trying to twist your arm, using bully-boy tactics?'

She nodded. There was no need to say a thing. He'd

been reviewing the scene in his mind, remembering body language, and had arrived at the right conclusion. She didn't want to talk about her ex-husband, not now, not ever. She was feeling far too guilty because of what she had agreed to do to want him inside her head.

But Jed didn't want to let it go. 'Speaking objectively, and having seen him, I can't understand why you ever married the man. You're an intelligent woman, Elena. Independent, fastidious.'

Knowing what she knew, that she was deceiving him over the payment of Liam's blackmailing demands, she wished he'd leave it, forget the other man had ever existed. But if there were things he wanted to know she'd tell him, because she owed him that. And his tone hadn't been censorious, just calmly, objectively questioning.

She traced a line in the condensation on the outside of her glass, amazed to find her hand was steady when her heart was punching her breastbone. 'He didn't always look like that, or act like a lout. He had a silver tongue, was very easy on the eye. He had the type of charm that could dazzle. I was gullible, easily flattered, overwhelmed by his lavish gifts—glitzy designer gowns, shoes made in heaven, jewellery. A bit flashy, not the sort of thing Nolan's would touch with a sanitised bargepole, but expensive nevertheless.' Her fingers worried at the corner of her mouth, and the way Jed fastened on that nervous betrayal, one brow drifting upwards, told her he knew how upset this conversation was making her.

She *was* upset—her deceit over those blackmail demands was doing her head in—but if she weren't careful he might think she was mourning the man her first husband had been.

She clamped both hands round her glass and forced herself on. 'After a time, it all began to pall—the fancy restaurants, the nightclubs, the feeling of being dressed up and paraded. And I came out from under his spell for long enough to question where all the money was coming from.

'Gambling, he told me. And that I wasn't happy about. Poor but honest—that was the way Mum had brought me up. And that was why I was so shocked when I discovered his criminal activities, why I went to the police. Why I divorced him. Now—' she looked at him from between her lashes, her eyes unconsciously pleading '—can we forget him?'

'With pleasure.' He was on his feet, collecting their belongings. 'Consider the subject permanently closed. Shall we head for the hills?'

She dragged in a shuddery breath, relief smoothing down her prickly nerve-ends. Whatever test he'd been setting for her, it seemed she'd passed with flying colours.

They'd reached Las Rocas in the late afternoon, Jed flinging the windows wide while Elena dealt with the shopping. They'd taken turns to shower and change, both careful not to force an intimacy too soon, not before the problems within their marriage had been resolved.

They'd been down that road on the night of the award ceremony and it had ended in unmitigated disaster.

And now, after a quickly prepared meal of garlicky

prawns, vegetable medley and masses of fruit, they were sprawled out on Siamese-twinned loungers, gazing out over the terrace at the vast starlit velvet night, the perfume from her pots of lilies and sweet-scented jasmine drugging the senses.

She'd felt so swelteringly hot and sticky when they'd arrived she'd thankfully exchanged the clothes she'd travelled in for cotton shorts and a loose, cropped and sleeveless top. Jed, too, had dressed lightly. The fine cotton, collarless black shirt hung from his rangy shoulders in soft folds, the sleeves pushed up above his elbows, his brief white shorts making those long, elegantly muscular legs look deeply tanned and unbelievably sexy in the mellow glow from the outside wall-lamps.

Quickly, Elena fixed her attention on the stars. The temptation to reach out and touch that bronzed skin was deeply compelling. Pictures of their former hedonistic lovemaking banded her brain, making her heart flutter, her mouth go dry.

'Do you mind if we talk?' From the corner of her eye she saw him turn onto his side, supporting his head with his hand. 'Look at me, Elena.'

She turned her head, obeying his soft command, her bright hair spread out on the reclining back-rest of the lounger. Starlight glimmered in his eyes, deep shadows emphasising the harsh hollows and planes of his face, making the line of his mouth tantalisingly sensual.

'OK?'

'Of course.' Her soft mouth quivered. This was the breakthrough; she knew it was. She was willing to tell him anything he wanted to know.

'I believe your story of artificial insemination. And, no, I didn't check with the clinic. They wouldn't have told me anything in any case. It would have been a gross breach of patient confidentiality. But the more I thought about it the more it made sense, fitted in with what I knew of Sam. Did you really want a child that badly?'

He hadn't taken his eyes off her face for a second, and she returned his steady gaze unflinchingly. 'Yes, I did,' she breathed. 'It was a physical ache that wouldn't go away. It got so bad it made everything I'd achieved in my life seem worthless.

'After my divorce I made a solemn vow never to marry again. I'd make my own life and make it good. That,' she whispered, 'was before I met you and knew how wrong I'd been. Sam wanted a child, too, but for him it was different, a kind of stake in the future, his sole claim to immortality. It was a cerebral need. Not, as mine was, a deep emotional hunger. It was almost as if he knew he didn't have long to live.'

Unconsciously, her hand covered her unborn child, the protective gesture as old as time. And Jed rolled closer and slid his hand beneath hers, moving it gently over her rounded tummy.

'Is this little bulge the result of gorging yourself at supper? Or is it what I think it is?' His voice was husky, heavy velvet, his dark head close to her bright one, his clean breath feathering over her face.

Elena pulled in a raggedy breath and moved, making enough space for him, just, on her lounger. If he'd a mind to avail himself of it.

He had, and, so close to him now she was sure he must hear the race of her heart as it pushed the blood wildly through her veins, she murmured, 'It's what you think it is.' She held her breath, because his reaction would tell her what their future was more plainly than any words. If he showed any sign of distaste then she'd know that he would always resent Sam's child, and the future wouldn't look hopeful.

He didn't say a word, simply undid the button at the top of the waistband of the shorts that were now just that little bit too tight, allowing his hand the freedom to dip lower.

Relief made her giddy for long seconds, and then desire pooled at the juncture of her thighs, sweet and sharp and urgent. Would his hand slide lower, touch her there? Did he want her half as much a she wanted him?

Would he let her into his heart again? Would he love her, let her love him?

'Jed—' she croaked, wanting to ask him, but he wouldn't let her finish, his voice sliding over hers.

'Once, at Netherhaye, you let slip that you still loved me. Then that night at the hotel you told me, most emphatically, that you didn't. Which version of the state of your emotions am I to believe?'

'The first.' She turned her head, resting her cheek against the angle of his shoulder, burning for him, loving him, loving him... 'We were so close to making love. I knew you'd despise yourself if you did. And despise me for letting you. You hated me, closed me out, wouldn't believe me! I had to do—say—something to stop us!'

She was rapidly losing her ability to control herself. The need to feel his hands on her body, his lips on hers, to curl herself round the hard male length of him, to feel him deep inside her, hear words of love on his lips again, was pushing her to the limits of her endurance.

The hand that had been softly stroking her tummy stilled. She held her breath, the fear of rejection surging back, a sour taste in her mouth, a cold stone in her heart. But he said thickly, 'Will you forgive me for that? Can you ever forgive me for that? For refusing to listen, and, when you forced me to listen, telling you you were a liar? For refusing to trust? I think I went half out of my mind at that time.'

'Oh, darling...' In answer, she wound her arm around his neck, her lips feathering his mouth as she told him, 'Of course I do! I understand how you must have felt. Had the positions been reversed I'd have behaved ten thousand times as badly!'

'I don't think I deserve you.' His voice was rough, but his hand was gentle as it moved on her tummy again, protectively gentle. 'But I promise you this. I will love this child as if it were my own. Not for Sam's sake, and not because I love its mother. But for its own sake.'

Emotional tears streaked her face and he kissed them lovingly away. She could feel the fine tremors that shook his taut body as he found her lips and parted them with his, and the last coherent thought she had was that Catherine had not been given the opportunity to wipe away those misconceptions of his about coming a poor second-best to his brightly burning, will o' the wisp brother.

He had put those aside himself. Dismissed ancient sibling jealousy and reclaimed his own.

This much loved—adored—husband of hers was an honourable man.

'You are so beautiful,' he told her, his voice raw with need. 'Let me show you how I love you.' He took her hands and lifted them, turned them, placed fervent kisses in the centre of each curled palm. Then he lifted his head. The lamplight gilded the skin that was pulled tightly over his bones, his smoky eyes locking intently with hers. 'Show me you forgive me.'

Emotion shook her; she couldn't speak. She wound her arms around his neck again and kissed him fiercely, and he returned her frenzy as, hands trembling, they tore the clothes from each other's bodies until flesh met burning flesh.

She heard him groan and curled her legs around his body, inviting him to enter her. She heard the slow, inward drag of his breath, saw his tough jaw tighten and knew a second's terrible fear that this was all going wrong, before he said raggedly, 'I'm wild for you, afraid of hurting you and the baby. Help me to love you gently.'

She melted against him and thought she was in paradise. Nothing else could have spelled out his love for her more perfectly.

'We'll make it as slow and long and lingering as you like, my darling,' she promised as he slid gently, slowly within her, and she wrapped her arms more tightly around him and *knew* she was in paradise.

CHAPTER ELEVEN

THE evening sun was low, spreading misty purple shadows in the valleys. Elena moved around the kitchen preparing supper. Sautéed clams with garlic and lemon, and parsley from her garden. Her eyes were inevitably drawn from the task in hand over the terrace, to where Jed was dragging the hose around the garden, dressed only in worn denim cut-offs and espadrilles.

A sensation that was near to pain clutched at her heart. Oh, dear heaven, how she loved this man! Over the two days they'd spent here the new intensity of their love had revealed itself in every touch, every caress, every look and every word. Their love for each other doubly precious because they had so nearly lost each other.

'Would you prefer it if we stayed here until the baby's born?' he'd asked her this morning as they'd stood on the terrace contemplating what needed to be done today in the rioting garden, not wanting to set foot outside their secluded paradise. His arms had come around her, pulling her into his body, his hands softly cradling her breasts through the gauzy aqua cotton of the loose sundress she'd been wearing over nothing at all.

'Would you mind?' She'd tipped her head back, nuzzling her lips against his throat, feeling the beat of his pulse, feeling her breasts swell invitingly beneath his tormenting hands.

'I'd prefer it. This place suits you, and it's certainly grabbed my affection. We could visit Netherhaye once in a while, just to keep the old place aired, and have Christmas there every year and invite the Mums. Because I've been thinking; I can just as easily keep an eye on the business from here. We could spend the bulk of our time here, making babies.' His voice had teased, taking every last one of her senses and giving them delight. 'Would you like that?'

She'd turned in his arms then, pushing herself against him, holding him to her heart, closing her eyes on a ragged breath as she'd felt his body stir with desire. 'I want to give you babies,' she'd told him, her voice ferocious with love. 'Dozens of them!'

And now this big-hearted man of hers was winding the hose back on its reel, and the play of muscles across his powerful back and shoulders mesmerised her, making her throat tighten with emotion. He was so beautiful.

And he would be hungry. He'd worked hard in the garden all afternoon, wanting her with him but not allowing her to do more than idly dead-head the blossoms. He was very determinedly taking care of her.

She finished tossing the salad as he straightened up from his task. He'd be with her in a matter of seconds. All the ingredients were ready; she could cook the clams while he had his shower.

The phone rang. She dried her hands and took the receiver from the wall-mount, and Liam said aggressively, 'You got it?'

Her heart stopped, then punched at her savagely.

'Where are you?' She'd gone cold all over, shaking. Everything had been so wonderful, Jed had been so perfect, so understanding, and she had put Liam and his demands to the back of her mind.

Now he was filling her head with panic. She wanted to put the receiver down, go on pretending he didn't exist.

'Close.' He answered her question. 'I'm looking at the front of your property right now. Nice place. Must be worth a bomb. So when and where do we meet?'

Her stomach was churning sickly, her brain in a tumult. But she had to think. And quickly. Jed would walk in at any moment.

She cast a wide-eyed, frantic glance at the door and said tightly, 'Then you will be able to see the big door in the wall. The package will be outside it tomorrow at dawn.' And she hooked the receiver back just as Jed walked through, and felt her face flood with guilty colour.

'You OK?' His eyes narrowed with concern. 'Who was on the phone—not bad news?'

She had to get herself together. Stop shaking. Look normal. She pulled in a deep breath, willed herself to carry this off.

'No, of course not. Just my agent reminding me I'm due to give my publishers a synopsis of my next book any time now,' she invented, hating having to do this, reminding herself that she was doing it for his sake, trying to feel better about it and failing miserably.

'Sweetheart…' He came closer, his easy smile making her want to weep. 'Don't let them pressure you.' He folded his arms around her and her head dropped gratefully against the wide span of his chest. His skin was warm, slick with sweat. She parted her lips, tasting him.

'You never need write another word,' he said firmly. 'Not unless you want to. And if you do, then you tell them you do it on your own time, at your own pace. That clear?'

He was making a stand for her, taking her side as she knew he always would. That it was inappropriate didn't matter a damn. He would shoulder her problems, deal with them fairly and firmly, always on her side.

She wound her arms around his neck and said fiercely, 'I love you!'

'Hey! You think I don't know that? That's why I'm here. That's why I married you, remember.' He was smiling as his lips took hers.

Very gently, Elena moved Jed's arm, holding her breath, afraid he would wake.

She hadn't slept, increasingly edgy as the hours of night slipped past her. Constantly reminding herself that she was doing this for his sake alone was the only way she could stop herself from breaking down and confessing everything.

He had slept, wrapped around her. His conscience hadn't been stinging, keeping him awake. Tomorrow—today, actually—they were going to Seville.

Over supper Jed had told her he was due to meet the designer he'd contracted to gut the present building and turn it into something discreetly impressive, glamorous yet restrained, the international hallmark of a Nolan's showroom.

'I'd like you to be involved—if only to give your opinions. Besides—' his eyes had glinted at her '—I want you with me. I can't bear to be away from you for a second, let alone the best part of a day.'

'You think I'd let you go without me!' She'd smiled for him, hanging onto the thought of the trip to Seville. By then the business with Liam would be over. He'd have taken his bundle of crisp notes and run. And she could put him out of her mind and get on with her wonderful life with Jed.

Gingerly sliding out of bed, she wondered if she'd be too sleepy to make any contribution to today's business meeting. And then told herself of course she wouldn't. Relief that this was all over would carry her through, make her bubble and bounce with sheer happiness.

The louvres were open, and she found her silk robe by the grey pre-dawn light, slipped it on, the fine fabric cool against her naked skin, and tied the belt with shaky fingers.

She was hardly daring to breathe, and her heart felt as if it had swollen to twice its normal size, bumping about inside her chest. But Jed was still sleeping. She slipped like a shadow from the room.

It would take no longer than three minutes—four at the most—to slip out with the package and get back into bed. And if he did wake during that time, find her missing, he'd assume she'd gone to the bathroom.

She'd deliberately left her handbag on top of the counter just inside the kitchen door, so she didn't need to put a light on to find it. Quickly, she reached for it, and knocked the salt and pepper grinders to the tiled floor. She cursed herself for forgetting they were there.

The noise sounded horrendous. Her fingers clutched the soft leather of her bag and her heart stopped beating, then thundered on as quietness settled around her.

He hadn't woken. She delved for the package and padded through the house, taking care not to bump into furniture. The main door was heavy, wide and ancient. Jed had shot the bolts home before going to bed. She reached for the top one, remembering the grinding noise it made. They both needed oiling.

She was sweating, rivers of panic rushing through her veins, when she finally pulled the door open and stepped outside into the enclosed courtyard at the front of the house.

All she had to do now was put the package outside the big arched doorway.

In contrast, those doors swung open easily, and she was on the stony track, the rosy fingers of dawn already touching the tops of the crumpled mountains. She bent to put the package down—and Liam stepped out of the shadows.

She slapped her hand across her mouth to push back her cry of fright, and dropped the package. Liam picked it up, weighing it in his hands. She hadn't expected him to be waiting. She hadn't wanted him to be waiting. She had never wanted to see him or speak to him again.

'Thanks, doll.' He grinned at her. 'You know it makes sense.'

He looked more respectable than when he'd appeared at Netherhaye. The dark grey denims and matching battle jacket looked new. And she could see a fancy truck parked a little way down the track. Had he borrowed it? Or stolen it? Either way, she didn't care. She wanted him off her property.

'Just go,' she hissed through her teeth, shivering now in the chilly dawn air.

'Only when I've checked this isn't a wad of newspaper.' He opened the package, pulling out the crisp notes. He leered at her. 'I'm not *au fait* with the exchange rate, but it looks about right to me. I don't think you'd be stupid enough to do the dirty on me again. It will do nicely, for starters.'

'There won't be any seconds,' she told him decisively, refusing to give in to the desire to have hysterics. 'So take it and go, and just be thankful I didn't go to the police and have you put behind bars again!'

She heard the opening of the door in the wall behind her and went weak with a totally unexpected surge of relief. She had tried, for his sake, to keep him ignorant of this vile business, but he had woken and followed her out so she had failed.

But this failure was sweetly welcome. She no longer had the need to deceive him. If Liam did go to the tabloids when she refused to make more payments— and Jed would insist she did nothing of the kind—then at least he would be forewarned, prepared when those smears against her character—and, by association, his—came to light.

'Get off this property, Forrester.' Jed's voice was hard and flat. 'If I see your face around here again I'll personally rearrange it for you.' The lack of emotion in his tone made the threat very real. Even Liam blinked as he hurriedly stuffed the paper money back into the package, as if he was afraid the other man would take it from him.

Turning swiftly, Elena hurried to Jed's side. He hadn't bothered to dress, just pulled on the cut-offs he'd worn the day before. She reached out a hand, her fingers light and cool on the firm, warm skin of his arm. 'Thank you,' she said huskily, and really, really meant it.

'Get back inside before you get a chill.' His eyes swept the inadequate silk that skimmed her naked body. He turned and walked through the arched doorway, waiting for her, then re-secured the double doors. He strode back to the house, straight to the bathroom. She stood outside the door, listening to the gushing of hot water, her heart quailing.

Surely he didn't think...

She pushed open the door just as he turned the shower head off. He reached for a towel, his eyes flat. 'I suggest you go back to bed. From the look of you, your furtive assignation obviously took it out of you. Funny thing is, if I hadn't cared I would never have known you'd told him where you'd be, arranged for him to come to you. What did you do? Promise to give him that hand-out because you felt sorry for him? Or because you like to keep men dangling? Can't you let him go?'

He was still using that flat, emotionless tone. That made it all so much worse. It couldn't all be going so wrong, not for a second time!

He finished with the towel and tossed it in a corner. 'As I said, if I hadn't cared I wouldn't have known. I heard noises, heard the bolts being drawn. I thought you couldn't sleep. So I followed. I didn't want you to be sleepless and alone. But you weren't alone.'

She knew how it must look. But she wasn't going

to stand by and see their lives ruined, their future together blown out of the water. 'Jed,' she said firmly
as he walked past her into the bedroom, careful not to
touch her, 'will you please listen to me?'

'No, thanks, I've done more than my fair share of
that.' He was dressing. A pale grey suit in a lightweight fabric, pale grey silk shirt and a dark tie. 'Trouble is, you're too good with make-believe. I suddenly
find I don't know what's truth and what's fantasy.' He
settled his jacket on his shoulders and glanced at his
watch. 'I may get back from Seville tonight. And,
there again, I may not.'

Elena sat on the edge of the bed and watched him
walk out, her eyes defeated, brimming with a sudden
rush of unstoppable tears.

This couldn't be happening all over again. Surely it
couldn't? Hadn't he learned from his earlier refusal to
listen to what she had to say?

Yet he had worked it out in his own good time,
weighing what seemed bad, very bad indeed, against
what he knew of her, the love they shared, and had
reached the truth.

On the other hand, perhaps seeing her with Liam
again had completely turned his opinion of her around.
That first meeting had been explained away, and he'd
come to accept it. But the second—the wad of money
that could only have come from her. The indisputable
fact that she had arranged to sneak out and meet her
ex-husband. Would he now see everything she'd said
as a tissue of deceitful lies? Even the way Sam's baby
had been conceived?

She spent the day alternating between faint hope
and bleak despair. He didn't come that night, nor in
the morning. But Pilar did.

CHAPTER TWELVE

ELENA knew she had to make herself eat something for her baby's sake. She was uninterestedly slicing fruit when she heard the unmistakable sound of a noisy two-stroke engine pull into the courtyard.

Pilar on her moped, come to check on the practically invisible irrigation system that kept the pot plants alive. It saved having to drag the hose or watering cans up to the terrace that overlooked the garden and the courtyard at the front.

Pilar always came to check the system was working properly at least once a week when Elena was away. Now the Spanish woman would know she was back in residence, and would expect to take up her normal household duties.

But Elena didn't want to see anyone. Only Jed. And Jed, it seemed, was in no hurry to come back.

Sighing, she resigned herself to the inevitable as the heavy slap of Pilar's sandalled feet heralded her arrival in the kitchen. A huge woman, she was full of good humour and energy. Elena liked her very much, and vowed not to let her know how desperately she wanted to be left alone.

'So you are having the baby—that is good! The little one will bring you much joy! I speak as I know from the five of my own!' Pilar said in her exuberant, heavily accented English.

Her eyes widening, Elena glanced down at the front

of her sundress. Another five months to go—was her pregnancy so obvious?

Pilar, taking a gaudy spotted pinafore from a plastic bag, tied it round her huge middle and disabused her. 'Señor Nolan called to tell me the good news and say you are back here now and I am needed.'

'When did he call? This morning?' Had he been in the village below, that close to her, and not bothered to come up here? Was he coldly and unemotionally cutting her out of his life again?

'No, no.' Pilar gave her a look that suggested she doubted her sanity. 'While I was making lunch yesterday. He asked in the village for the house of Pilar Casals. Now you see I was right to make you talk to me in English all these years! Señor Nolan has no Spanish, but we were able to understand each other.'

Which was more than Elena did at this moment. Jed should have been in Seville by yesterday lunchtime. But Pilar gave her no time to ponder why he hadn't been, telling her, 'And Tomás is to come and water the garden and do other heavy work. That is good for all of us. He is on his way now, on his bicycle. I tell him my old motorbike won't take my weight and his. Are you going to eat that fruit, or shall I make the good *tortilla*?'

'Fruit,' Elena said weakly, resuming her slicing before Pilar could make good her threat.

She could understand Pilar's elation very well. Her husband, Tomás, only worked when Pilar forced him to, and would happily sit around all day at one of the pavement cafés down in the village, drinking strong coffee and smoking his evil-smelling cigarillos under the shade of an orange tree, reading the papers and talking to his friends, perfectly content to let his wife work to put food on the table for the family. She would be delighted to know he would be bringing in extra income.

When Pilar began clattering round with the mop and bucket Elena took her fruit to eat in the garden under the shade of a giant fig tree. Pilar would fetch her if Jed phoned. Though she had by now stopped hoping that he would.

Responsibly, he had arranged for her to have all the help around the house and garden she needed, and had probably told Pilar to see she ate properly. He had done his duty by her and his brother's unborn child. He would want little or no further contact.

By the end of the afternoon the ache in her heart had become permanent, the feeling of loss so acute it was difficult to contain. Surely his business in Seville wasn't keeping him away this long? If he'd meant to return he would have done so by now. She had a thumping headache from listening for the sound of his car.

Tomás had set off back to the village on his rusty old bicycle, and Pilar was heading through the court-yard, pushing her moped, on her way home, turning to call over her shoulder, 'I have made you Pollo con Tomate; be sure you eat it.'

Standing in the doorway, Elena made herself smile and promise to eat the chicken in tomato sauce. She didn't want the Spanish woman to guess how despairingly unhappy she was.

Then she heard the sound of an approaching engine and her smile turned to one of wobbly relief. He had come back!

Her legs turned to something resembling water vapour and she sagged back against the doorframe, her stomach full of nervous flutters as she saw him appear in the arched doorway in the outer wall. Even though her eyes were misted with emotion she could see how drawn he looked, how tired. He stopped and exchanged a few words with Pilar, then walked towards her, the severity of his expression enclosing her rapidly beating heart in ice.

Nothing had changed in the last thirty-six hours.

He walked past her, into the coolness of the hall. She followed. At the entrance to the sitting room he made a curt after-you gesture with one hand. 'Shall we talk?'

It was what she wanted, but her heart was somewhere under the soles of her feet, heavy and aching. The coldness of his voice, his eyes, everything about him, told her he was about to say something she couldn't bear to hear.

She clung to the back of a chair for support. Her legs were shaking so badly. He put his briefcase down on a table and told her, 'As you'll have gathered, the Casalses will give you all the help you need around here. And I spoke to Catherine last night and told her you'd decided to wait here until the birth. It is your home, the place you'll feel most comfortable in.'

He pushed his hands in his pockets and turned to stare out of the open windows, as if he'd seen enough of her. 'I'll be flying out to New York tomorrow and staying for four weeks, maybe five. I'll let you know. After that I'll check up on you from time to time, and nearer the birth I'll be with you. We'll book into a hotel in Cadiz. I've checked out a private maternity unit on the outskirts, and booked you in. I'm sure,' he said coldly, 'you went into the logistics of getting proper prenatal care when you first decided you wanted a child.'

She'd listened to him outlining his plans for their sterile future, the unemotional delivery of the words stunning her into silence. But now she blurted anguishedly, 'Jed! Don't do this to us!'

He turned then. Slowly. His eyes were empty, as if no one lived behind them. 'My dear,' he drawled, 'I don't believe I'm the one doing anything to "us."'

He shifted his attention to the briefcase on the table, opening it, pulling out an all too familiar package. 'This is yours. I hope you'll dispose of it more sensibly next time. When I left here yesterday morning,' he said in a terse explanation, when he met her puzzled stare, 'I scoured the village and found his vehicle outside that run-down-looking *pension*. Considering the earliness of your assignation, I thought he might be staying nearby. I persuaded him to hand this back.' He dropped the package on the table with a look of mild distaste. 'And I hope it won't come as too much of a disappointment, but you won't be seeing or hearing from him again. I got the message over to him in a way that not even he could misunderstand.'

He snapped the briefcase shut. 'I'll phone you from New York.' And he walked out.

Elena let him go. There was no point in following him, arguing, pleading. Jed Nolan had made up his mind and there was nothing she could do or say that would alter it.

He phoned from New York, faithfully each week. Elena's despair turned to hopelessness, and then to dull apathy. His questions were bluntly to the point, and it was all she could do to drag out her responses.

She was well. She had regular appointments with her gynaecologist in Cadiz. Yes, she had visited the maternity unit. And that was it; that was all.

If his phone calls depressed her then his first visit did more than that. He arrived at noon, cool in a loose white cotton shirt, lightweight oyster-coloured trousers. The heat of the summer made her sweat, her hair flop lankily around her face. She felt fat and ugly and didn't want to see him.

He left when Pilar did, and she curled up on the sofa and cried until she felt sick. She felt as if someone had dug a deep, dark pit, thrown her in and covered her up. She didn't think she would ever climb out of it again, didn't think she wanted to.

On his second visit, exactly a month later, he left well before Pilar. The Spanish woman was beside herself with excitement. 'Señor Nolan is such a good man! See how he cares about you!' Her black eyes rolled expressively. 'Sadly, his business takes him so much away. But—' she could hardly contain herself '—last time he say to us he is buying a car. For us. Yesterday it came. A new car, not an old thing. For our own. But for Tomás to drive you wherever you need to go. First he needed to satisfy himself Tomás is safe. That one, I told him, is very safe for driving. Too lazy to drive faster than a snail! One car we had once, in our early days. Then it fell to bits and now the hens live in it in the back yard.'

He was doing his duty. He was good at that. She dreaded his next visit. Next month she would be huger than ever. She hated him seeing her like this. Fat. Dull. Lifeless. Dreaded the polite questions on the state of her health. Was she eating enough? Eating the right things, getting plenty of rest?

He'd brought little snippets of news—very little about what *he* was doing and where he was doing it, mainly about how well Catherine and Susan were settling in their cottage, digging up the entire garden, apparently, and replanting, haunting sale rooms and antiques shops for just the right pieces of furniture. So he had to have visited Netherhaye, spent some time there.

The two ladies had threatened to fly out to visit her, but, Jed had told her, he had dissuaded them, telling them she was busy on a new book. Was she writing?

Mutely, she had shaken her head. She was doing nothing but managing to get through each day. Sometimes even that seemed too much to cope with.

She knew now, without him having to tell her, that after the birth he would go for divorce. Catherine was back on her feet, had a new life to make in a new home, plenty to keep her occupied. There was no need now to stay married.

Oddly enough, she accepted it, had come to understand him better.

He was nothing if not an honourable man, a man who took duty and responsibility seriously—she only had to witness the care he had extended to her, albeit from a distance, to know that.

A man of his word. He would have nothing but contempt for a wife who consistently presented him with what he could only view as deceit.

He might have loved her once. She knew he had. But he couldn't stay with her.

Not even for great sex.

Not even for a true and loving heart?

The parcel of tiny baby clothes arrived from England when the winds of early October carried the first hint of autumn chill through the mountains. Elena's heart came out of deep-freeze.

The parcel had come from Catherine and her mother, and she dialled the number Jed had given her and spoke to them both. It was Catherine who said, 'I'm glad to hear you're sounding better. You got me worried, you sounded so flat when we phoned last. I even suggested to Jed when he was over here a few weeks ago that Susan and I might visit and cheer you up. You must be missing him so—I can't think why he doesn't make someone else do all these foreign trips.'

'These lovely things have cheered me up,' Elena said, and meant it. So far she had done nothing to prepare for her baby.

'And you remember what we talked about back in early summer? About the way I tended to spoil Sam and why? Well, I did get to have that talk with Jed.' Catherine gave a fluttery half-laugh. 'And do you know what he said? He said he'd worked that out for himself, and that it had helped in a certain situation. I can't think what he meant, and he wouldn't tell me. Anyway, I'm glad I got it said.'

She knew what he'd meant, Elena thought sadly, after ending the conversation five minutes later. Jed had thought things through. He'd believed what she'd told him about her baby's conception, accepted that he didn't come second-best to his brother, accepted that he had no reason to doubt that he came first with her, and always would.

Until what had happened with Liam had changed all that, made him question her integrity all over again, question his own judgement of her character, weigh up the facts as they were known to him and find her wanting.

It was the worst thing that had happened to her, but she had to accept that he would never change his opinion back again. So she had Pilar and Tomás help her turn the bedroom with the south-facing windows into a nursery, decorating it in soft shades of cream and primrose-yellow. Then she organised a day out for them all.

They did it in style, all dressed in their best. She and Pilar in the back of the car—Pilar gave a great shout of laughter. 'You and I together, we will break the springs!'—and Tomás proudly in front, dressed in a shiny blue suit, driving, Elena was sure, with the brakes on most of the time.

By the time they'd toured the stores and baby boutiques, ordered everything from a crib to a fluffy bear, they were flagging. Elena treated them to lunch, surprised to find herself hungry, enjoying herself.

So life went on, and it was early November, the nights cold enough now for huge fires made from the logs Tomás split daily.

Soon, she supposed, Jed would put in an appearance, and, nearer the time of the birth, whisk them off to wait in one of the hotels in Cadiz, to be near the maternity unit. He had given his word and he would keep it. No matter how difficult it would be for both of them; no matter if seeing him again resurrected the awful, keening pain in her heart.

He came on a black night of torrential rain. She heard him call her name and willed her heart to keep beating calmly, not to panic, not to ache, and most of all not to fruitlessly yearn for what could never be again.

She hauled herself out of the chair where she'd been watching the dancing flames and listening to the wind howling in the chimneys, and smoothed down the smothering smock she was wearing over maternity leggings. She resolutely refused to let herself feel embarrassed by the way she looked.

Her hands rested on the shelf that had once been her waist. This was her baby, her life. He wanted no part in either. She had to remember that. When he walked into the cosy, comfy room, the heavy curtains closed to shut out the wild night, she said, 'I think you should turn round and go straight back before the road gets impassable.'

Although he had visited occasionally since he'd discovered her with Liam he had never stayed overnight. She doubted he would want to, even if she suggested it. 'In weather like this there can be rock falls, and the road down to the village turns into a river.' He looked haunted, she saw, hollow-eyed with weight loss. She didn't dare show she cared. 'There's no need for you to be here.'

'I see the need,' he said harshly, as if that was all that mattered. He strode further into the room, shrugged off his rain-darkened soft suede coat and dropped it on the floor. His black cashmere sweater clung to the wide bones of his shoulders. His eyes raked her, eyes that burned with the emotion that had been missing for months.

'One.' He came closer. 'You shouldn't be alone here in weather like this. Two.' He came close enough to touch her if he'd wanted to. 'I need to be here. With you. I can't stay away. Don't ask me to.'

Elena's brow wrinkled, her eyes searching his face. What she saw was fierce intent and something else, something soft and lost that looked like pleading. Did he mean his sense of responsibility, the duty of care he felt towards her and Sam's unborn child, wouldn't let him rest when he knew she'd be alone at night after Pilar and Tomás had left?

Or did he mean something else?

'I don't understand.' Her mouth felt unmanageable. The niggling backache she'd had all day suddenly became a ferocious spasm. She swallowed a gasp, waited until it had passed, then sank down again onto her chair.

Immediately he hunkered down in front of her. 'Are you all right?'

'Perfectly.' His hair was wet, rumpled. She wanted to run her fingers through it—wouldn't let herself, of course.

He gave her a searching look and then, as if satisfied, stood upright, fed more logs onto the fire, then began to pace.

'I put you on a pedestal,' he told her with almost savage self-contempt. 'I had no right to do that. No one's perfect.' He swung round and smiled thinly. 'Not even me. Especially not me. I believed what you told me about the baby. Not because I checked your story, because I didn't. But when I'd cooled down my heart told me you were telling the truth. Then that business with Forrester cropped up and muddied the waters, and I didn't know what to believe.'

He was staring into the fire again, one arm draped across the stone mantel, when the next contraction came. Elena sucked in her breath and ignored it. This was more important.

'I had no damned right to let that happen,' he said rawly. 'If you felt sorry for him—you had been his wife and you must have loved him once—and wanted to help him get back on his feet, then I had no right to prevent you, to get violently jealous because you still had a residue to feeling left for him.'

Silently, Elena got to her feet, her hands pressed into the small of her back. The contractions were coming strongly now, quickly. But before she said anything about it, did anything about it, she had to know. 'Are you suggesting we try again—to make this marriage work?'

'Not try.' He turned to her, his eyes burning. 'It *will* work—if you can forgive me.'

'Why now?' she asked thickly, not daring to let herself believe in this sudden change of heart. 'It's been almost four months. You stayed away. And even when you made those duty visits we might as well have been on different planets.'

'You think I don't know that. You think it didn't tear me apart?' His eyes were tortured. He spread his hands. 'Do you think I don't know what a fool I've been? I can't bear life without you, Elena. I need to be with you, I love you, dammit!'

This was Jed, her Jed. Showing the emotions he'd

battened down. His flaws were all too human, as were hers. His strengths were what mattered, and she would match them with her own. She would find the courage to accept what he was saying. She moved towards him and put her hands on his shoulders.

'I love you. I never stopped. Loving you hurt, but it never stopped.'

The hands that reached for her, held her, were unsteady, his kiss tender, infinitely loving. 'I want to hold you for ever,' he said thickly. 'I've always regarded myself as being ultra-sensible, but with you my emotions rule my head. I'd have said all of this much sooner—months ago—but I was afraid I'd blown it, that you'd tell me I'd had my chance and wouldn't get another. I want you to promise that the next time I behave like a cretin you'll hit me with something heavy.'

'Promise,' she concurred breathlessly. 'If you'll do something for me.'

'Anything.'

She couldn't doubt his fervour. 'Phone Tomás and ask him to bring Pilar up right away. She's had five babies, and helped deliver dozens more.'

A tiny moment of shock, then he said quickly, 'The baby's coming?'

She nodded. 'A couple of weeks early.'

'Get your things. I'll drive you,' he told her firmly, taking charge. But she knew better.

'There won't be time.' She touched his arm. 'Phone Pilar.' She rode the next contraction, sweat dewing her face. She hadn't thought it would happen so quickly.

He gave her a brief but searching look and strode out of the room. He was back in moments.

'They're on their way. Also a doctor and midwife from the maternity unit.' He took her hand. 'Everything's going to be fine. You're not to worry.'

She clung tightly to his fingers. The doctor and midwife wouldn't be here in time, but everything *would* be fine as long as Jed was with her. 'You do love me?' she gasped, her eyes darkening with the ferocity of the contractions that were coming so close together now. 'That's the only thing that might worry me.'

'More than my life!' He cupped her face with his hands. 'I've never stopped. Whatever happens, I'll always love you. You have to believe that.'

She did, oh, she did! She smiled for him radiantly. 'That goes for me, too. So the only problem we have is how to get me to the bedroom.'

'Easy.' His face soft with loving concern, he lifted her in his arms and carried her there, and laid her gently on the bed.

'And not even out of breath,' she teased. 'A man who can carry something the size of a baby elephant has to be hero material!' She heaved herself to her feet again. 'It's better that I keep walking. Help me into a robe, would you, Jed?'

He did, loving care in everything he did, and she caught the tiny flicker of relief in his eyes when Pilar stumped into the room, carrying an armful of towels. She lifted her hand and touched the side of his face. 'Everything's going to be fine.'

'Naturally!' Pilar said firmly. 'It happens all time! Tomás is boiling water.' Her eyes didn't leave Elena; she was timing contractions. She nodded her head briskly. 'I collect things we need. Soon you will want to push. I will be back.'

Soon, very soon now. Elena knew it. 'There's something you should know, my darling. About Liam—'

'Shush.' He laid a finger across her lips, his eyes soft. 'He doesn't matter. If you're concerned about him, and want to help him get back on his feet, I'll track him down and return the money. I had no right to take it from him in the first place.'

'No,' she huffed. 'Will you listen to me for once?' Physical pain didn't make her feel sorry for herself; it made her cross. 'I didn't give him the equivalent of ten thousand pounds because I wanted to, dammit! It was what he demanded. Blackmail. Hand it over—' she panted '—or he'd blacken my name through the tabloids. And by—association—yours—and Nolan's. I knew you'd say let—let him do his worst. I didn't want that. Didn't mind about me. Did about you. Kept it from you. Hated it. Oh, my God!'

Her baby was very anxious to be born. Pilar was there. She took over. Helped her to the bed. It was all happening. Jed held her hand, stroked her forehead, murmured reassurances and loving words of praise.

Then he said, with a catch in his voice, 'This baby is like its father. Impatient. Sam's child. Sam could never contain himself, even when he was very young. If he wanted to do something he wanted to do it *now*. Wanted to climb a particular tree, then he'd hare right up it. Wanted to see if he could climb up on the roof to see if the chimneys were wide enough for Santa to climb down, then off he'd set. My parents had to watch him all the time; that's why he wasn't sent away to school.' He refreshed the cloth he'd been using to cool her brow in a bowl of lavender water. 'Physically, he was a weak child. But he had enough spirit for ten. Left to his own devices he'd have burned himself out.'

'You didn't mind?' she managed, hanging onto his hand, sure she was mangling it.

'For a time, yes, I did mind. I believed I'd been pushed out in favour of the new baby. Frankly, I resented him. Right up until I was around fifteen or sixteen. By that time I was able to understand more. And you were right. When I knew you were carrying Sam's child the old resentment did come back. But not for long. I was wrong—about him, about Liam,' he said quickly. 'If I'd known the creep was blackmailing you I'd have done a damn sight more than get your money back and threaten him.'

Elena didn't hear any more. Jed loved her, truly loved her, and all was right with her world. And she had a job to do, a great big whopping one by the feel of it.

And fifteen minutes later her baby daughter lay in her arms. Nine lusty pounds, with blue eyes and a mass of fine blonde hair.

'She looks exactly like you. She even has your stubborn chin!' Jed uncurled the tiny fingers. 'And before you ask, no, I don't give a damn if she isn't biologically mine. In every other way she is, and always will be. Yours and mine.'

Samantha Nolan's sturdy legs were working like pistons as she climbed the last of the steps up from the garden. She'd been helping Tomás water the flowers and her dungarees were soaked.

And she'd got mud in her hair. She liked Tomás, and Pilar. She liked everything except spinach.

Mummy said she'd like that when she was grown up. Samantha didn't think so. When it got to nearly winter she'd be four, and quite grown up.

She stopped to stick her bright head in a pot of scarlet geraniums. The spicy smell made her sneeze. She liked that, too.

She stumped up the final steps. Now she was going to teach her twin brothers to talk. They were nearly one year old, so it was time they did. Then she'd teach them to read, and draw proper pictures.

They were crawling all over the terrace, blue-clad rumps in the air, under the watchful eye of Mummy and Daddy. Mummy and Daddy were lying on the loungers that they always pushed together, and holding hands again.

They were always holding hands and cuddling. Samantha didn't mind that, so long as she got her share. She loved them very, very much. Ignoring her babbling, wriggling little brothers, she flew over the terrace and hurled herself into two pairs of loving arms.

HARLEQUIN PRESENTS®

Passion™

Looking for stories that *sizzle?* Wanting a read that has a little extra *spice?*

Harlequin Presents® is thrilled to bring you romances that turn up the *heat!*

This month look out for
The Marriage Surrender by Michelle Reid
Harlequin Presents #2014, March 1999

Every other month throughout 1999 there'll
be a Harlequin **PRESENTS PASSION** book by one of
your favorite authors.

In May 1999 don't miss
The Millionaire's Mistress by Miranda Lee
Harlequin Presents #2026

Pick up a Harlequin **PRESENTS PASSION**—
*where **seduction** is guaranteed!*

If you enjoyed what you just read,
then we've got an offer you can't resist!

Take 2 bestselling
love stories FREE!

Plus get a FREE surprise gift!

Clip this page and mail it to Harlequin Reader Service®

IN U.S.A.	IN CANADA
3010 Walden Ave.	P.O. Box 609
P.O. Box 1867	Fort Erie, Ontario
Buffalo, N.Y. 14240-1867	L2A 5X3

YES! Please send me 2 free Harlequin Presents® novels and my free surprise gift. Then send me 6 brand-new novels every month, which I will receive months before they're available in stores. In the U.S.A., bill me at the bargain price of $3.12 plus 25¢ delivery per book and applicable sales tax, if any*. In Canada, bill me at the bargain price of $3.49 plus 25¢ delivery per book and applicable taxes**. That's the complete price and a savings of over 10% off the cover prices—what a great deal! I understand that accepting the 2 free books and gift places me under no obligation ever to buy any books. I can always return a shipment and cancel at any time. Even if I never buy another book from Harlequin, the 2 free books and gift are mine to keep forever. So why not take us up on our invitation. You'll be glad you did!

106 HEN CNER
306 HEN CNES

Name	(PLEASE PRINT)	
Address	Apt.#	
City	State/Prov.	Zip/Postal Code

* Terms and prices subject to change without notice. Sales tax applicable in N.Y.
** Canadian residents will be charged applicable provincial taxes and GST.
 All orders subject to approval. Offer limited to one per household.
 ® are registered trademarks of Harlequin Enterprises Limited.

PRES99   ©1998 Harlequin Enterprises Limited

HARLEQUIN PRESENTS®

THE BARONS

One sister, three brothers— who will inherit, and will they all find lovers?

Jonas is approaching his eighty-fifth birthday, and he's decided it's time to choose the heir of his sprawling ranch, Espada. He has three ruggedly good-looking sons, Gage, Travis and Slade, and a beautiful stepdaughter, Caitlin.

Who will receive Baron's bequest? As the Baron brothers and their sister discover, there's more at stake than Espada. For love also has its part to play in deciding their futures....

Enjoy Gage's story:
Marriage on the Edge
Harlequin Presents #2027, May 1999

And in August, get to know Travis a whole lot better in
More than a Mistress
Harlequin Presents #2045

Available wherever Harlequin books are sold.

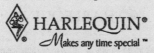

HARLEQUIN®
Makes any time special ™

Harlequin is proud to introduce:

HEART OF THE WEST

...Where Every Man Has His Price!

Lost Springs Ranch was famous for turning young mavericks into good men. Word that the ranch was in financial trouble sent a herd of loyal bachelors stampeding back to Wyoming to put themselves on the auction block.

This is a brand-new 12-book continuity, which includes some of Harlequin's most talented authors.

Don't miss the first book, **Husband for Hire** by Susan Wiggs. It will be at your favorite retail outlet in July 1999.

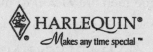

Coming Next Month

HARLEQUIN PRESENTS®

THE BEST HAS JUST GOTTEN BETTER!

#2043 TO BE A HUSBAND Carole Mortimer
Bachelor Brothers
It's the first time for Jonathan that any woman has resisted his charm. What does he have to do to win over the cool, elegant Gaye Royal? Propose marriage? But being a husband is the last thing Jonathan has in mind....

#2044 THE WEDDING-NIGHT AFFAIR Miranda Lee
Society Weddings
As a top wedding coordinator, Fiona was now organizing her ex-husband's marriage. But Philip wasn't about to let their passionate past rest. Then Fiona realized that Philip's bride-to-be didn't love him...but Fiona still did!

#2045 MORE THAN A MISTRESS Sandra Marton
The Barons
When Alexandra Thorpe won the eligible Travis Baron for the weekend, she didn't claim her prize. Travis is intrigued to discover why the cool blond beauty had staked hundreds of dollars on him and then just walked away....

#2046 HOT SURRENDER Charlotte Lamb
Zoe was enraged by Connel's barefaced cheek! But he had the monopoly on sex appeal, and her feelings had become so intense that Zoe couldn't handle him in her life. But Connel always got what he wanted: her hot surrender!

#2047 THE BRIDE'S SECRET Helen Brooks
Two years ago, Marianne had left her fiancé, Hudson de Sance, in order to protect him from a blackmailer. But what would happen now Hudson had found her again, and was still determined to marry her?

#2048 THE BABY VERDICT Cathy Williams
Jessica was flattered when Bruno Carr wanted her as his new secretary. She hadn't bargained on falling for him—or finding herself pregnant with his child. Bruno had only one solution: marriage!